Daisy Daring

And the Quest For the Loomis Gang Gold

Dennis Webster

North Country Books
Utica, New York

Daisy Daring
And the Quest For the Loomis Gang Gold

Copyright © 2005
by Dennis Webster

ISBN 1-59531-005-3

Library of Congress Cataloging-in-Publication Data

Webster, Dennis, 1966-
  Daisy Daring and the quest for the Loomis Gang gold / by Dennis
Webster.
    p. cm.
  ISBN 1-59531-005-3 (alk. paper)
  1. Librarians--Fiction. 2. New York (State)--Fiction. 3.
Treasure-troves--Fiction. I. Title.
  PS3623.E396D35 2005
  813'.6--dc22

                                        2005028294

Front Cover Design and Daisy Daring portrait by
Christine Martin
cmartin@fostermartin.com

North Country Books, Inc.
311 Turner Street
Utica, New York 13501
ncbooks@adelphia.net

To Kelly, Ashley, Jakob and Stephanie.
I'll love you forever.

Acknowledgments

There are so many people to thank in the creation of this book that I don't know if I can even list them all:

Evelyn Webster and Linda Gigliotti—the first readers of all my writings.

Lou Damelio for his reading and fantastic feedback.

Mike Laddin who has given me copious amounts of writing advice.

Steven Torres and Denny Griffin—thanks for the friendship my fellow mystery writers.

E. Fuller Torrey, M.D. for his gripping non-fiction book on the Loomis Gang.

Christine Martin for the striking painting of Daisy Daring and the snazzy front cover design.

Cindy Venettozzi for making my website.

Darlene DeSiato for reading an early draft and for her honest input.

Rob Igoe, Zach Steffen, Sheila Orlin and the rest of the excellent staff at North Country Books for giving Daisy a home.

The Utica Writer's Club for the encouragement and friendship.

Pho Mekong—N19 for making the best Chicken Noodle Soup in Utica.

The Central Association for the Blind and Visually Impaired for inspiring me to be a better person every day.

David Dowd for being almost as bad a fisherman as I am.

Craig Rippon for the writing and artistic discussions.

Don O'Hagan for his friendship.

& all the friends and family that have supported me. I love and thank you all.

Table of Contents

Chapter 1

Daisy Daring

I'm not a killer, but I wanted my library. I had pulled the switchblade out of my cowboy boot and pushed the button, snapped the blade into position, wiped the sweat from my brow with the back of my hand. I grabbed the rope and started sawing with all my might. I could feel the blood gurgling beneath my makeshift patch, my wound burning like St. Elmo's fire. I really didn't want to do that, but I had no choice. The backstabber should never have touched Doodle.

*   *   *

Shane Loomis

"You got a book on that war and stuff?"
"Do you know the title or author?"
"Uh-uh."
"What war is it?"
"You know, THE war."
I pointed out the history section and shook my head at the clueless youth who had come into the Waterville Public Library.

I was rubbing the thumbprints off the lenses of my glasses with my Johnny Cash concert shirt when I heard the cowbell on the door clank again, awakening Doodle from his sleeping purr, causing him to skeedadle under the biography section in the far corner of the library. I put my glasses back on and picked up my head in time to see a young man and even younger girl approaching the counter. He

1

didn't look to be the educated type, more like the standard teenage punk, with his too-tight tank top and a chain hanging off his hip. The girl wore a too-small top that barely covered her torso. Her bottom lip was pierced with a golden hoop and her over-bleached hair showed its sable roots. They weren't the library kind. I never remembered seeing them in here before but then most kids look alike to me.

"You're the smart lady, right? Your dad was the teacher who knew about my family history," he said. He took a comb out of his back pocket and ran it through his boot black hair while his companion was chewing away on a wad of cherry bubble gum. I could smell it ten feet away. The girl was nodding her head while pulling the gum out of her mouth, stretching it down past her chin.

"What can I do for you?" I closed my text on the pre-Socratics, leaving Anaxamander mid-sentence. I was engrossed in his theory of the undetermined, the Aperion—the unlimited. His fragment, "the unlimited is the first principle of things that are," rattles in my mind. I clasped my hands as if in prayer.

"My name is Shane Loomis. I heard you're an expert on the Loomis Gang and I need you to figure this out." He took what appeared to be a piece of yellowed parchment out of his pocket and laid it flat on the counter. I bent over and realized it wasn't paper at all, but a hairless animal skin. On it was strange writing that resembled calligraphy. I thought about how the ancient druids had written text on the hides of animals. I paused because I thought I recognized the script, although I had no idea exactly what it said.

My heart skipped when I realized it was written in the code of Wash Loomis, the leader of the notorious Loomis Gang. My father had shown me Wash's writing once. The calligraphy was done in a uncial style that was common a few centuries ago. I think it was related to a version of Esperanto that my father had researched most of his life. I remembered him dabbling in this writing, although I didn't know what tribe it belonged to. I knew that my father could read this if he were still alive.

There had always been rumors that Wash had written down the location of the Loomis Gang treasure; however, everyone assumed the map was destroyed in the big fire.

This young man was right. I knew more about the Loomis activities, how their network of two hundred members terrorized upstate New York up until the Civil War, than most people. For example, I knew that Wash was very secretive and had a map drawn up that showed the way to the gang's buried treasure. Could this yellowed skin be it?

"Well, rumor has it that Wash came back from the West Coast with a wooden chest full of gold. The chest is rumored to have been hidden in an underground tunnel to thwart thieves; a skeleton was laid across its top. Pirates were superstitious, they wanted the spirit of the dead man to protect their booty—a ghostly security guard of sorts. Shane jumped in with, "He supposedly hid the treasure on the Loomis property deep into Nine Mile Swamp. Quite possibly it's still in the same place."

My father did tell me that Wash Loomis had come back from the West with a trunk holding what he claimed he had stolen from simple miners. The gold could be anywhere in the poisonous Nine Mile Swamp. For over a hundred years no one had ever come close to finding it; thus the legend began. I know, much like Troy, that there's usually a pebble of truth in a mountain of fairy tales. There were many other legends where the gold came from. The Loomis legend was only one of many, but it still garnered some attention.

I knew that Shane Loomis was the sole remaining descendent of the educated but brutal Loomis Gang.

I picked up the slick skin, holding it up to the overhead lighting to see if it was real. I eyeballed the brown calligraphy that had cracked with time. For all I knew this could be nothing more than insane scribbling. It could be a false path into the Nine Mile Swamp, into quicksand, or nothing at all. "I wonder what kind of animal this was? Perhaps rabbit?"

"That's an animal skin?" said the girl. "That's sick. Writing on a living thing is wrong. I'm glad we've evolved into writing on something that's not a living thing; like paper."

"It's the pelt of an animal all right. I think it's a woodchuck," Shane answered.

"Well, I might be able to help you with this."

"Hot damn!" he yelled. His voice echoed off the walls, disturb-

3

ing Snider who was in the back corner reading the *Crabtree Courier's* comic section. Shane's icy blue eyes were ablaze and his hair was falling wildly about his face. He felt the need to comb it again.

"Shhhh." I held my index finger up to my dry lips. "You'll have to leave this with me and come back tomorrow."

"I told you," said the girl, in a snotty tone. She crossed her arms. She was tapping her foot as she snapped her gum. "She doesn't even look like a librarian. Why should we leave it with her? What makes you think we can trust her?"

"Lady, don't go thinking about doing anything without me. What's written on that skin is mine," warned Shane. "If there's anything worth anything in that letter, I'm the only one you tell, unless Jessica is with me, he quietly added. "You know what I mean?" He took the pen chained to the counter and wrote his name and phone number on the inside cover of my textbook, exposing a tattooed ring of thorns around his middle finger. Normally, defacing a text would get someone barred from the Waterville Public Library; however, I wasn't about to do that with a possible treasure map under my fingertips.

"I will try my best to see what I can figure out by tomorrow. It could take a little longer," I said. I took the unlit cigar, that I gnaw on for comfort, from my mouth and pointed it at them. "This should remain a secret, because you know the attention this could draw. I'm just saying we should be discreet."

"Sounds good to me. I'll be back tomorrow," promised Shane. He walked out of the library with his arm around his girl, his hand shoved deep in her back pocket. I didn't think they were married because there was no ring on either one of their ring fingers.

"You okay, Ms. Daring?" asked Snider. He had come from the back upon hearing Loomis shout. Snider was old and not a little deaf, so I wasn't worried. Even if he did hear the conversation I doubt he could make heads or tails of it.

"I'm fine, Snider." I spread my fingers and held my hand up to the light wondering what an engagement ring would look like. I mean, if I were ever to get one. I came close once.

Doodle had returned and jumped up onto the skin, laid down on it and began purring, choosing to become acquainted with the new animal arrival at the library. I rubbed his arching back and brushed the clump of orange fur into my garbage pail.

Snider was lingering behind me, quietly mumbling, but with the ringing telephone, I could barely hear him. I excused myself from our conversation by holding up my finger and running to the desk.

"Hello, Waterville Public Library. How may I help you?"

"I'm looking for a man with no arms and no legs. He hangs on the wall and goes by the name Art."

The young boy was joined in the background by other laughing voices.

"You better stop doing this before I trace the call. I'm serious." They hung up.

I shook off the prank phone call and pulled my father's gold-plated pocket watch out of the front pocket of my brown leather pants. I only had another hour before I could lock the library door and review this document a little more closely. I gently moved Doodle off the laid out skin. I folded it and put it into a manila envelope, hiding it under the counter so no one would see it.

The people of the Mohawk Valley have been obsessed with the missing gold of the Loomis Gang for the last century—I among them. We've had fortune seekers arrive in Waterville every few years thinking they had the way to the treasure. They'd go home bloody, scratched, bug-bitten, and defeated from the impassable Nine Mile Swamp. A few had gone in and never returned. It was rumored that the poisonous gas blocked the sun, making it more difficult to see where you were going. The acid air was thought to cause delirium and the gobs of molasses-like quicksand would pull you under. I always pictured villains clutching the air like in those Tarzan movies, until their last patch of flesh was sealed over by the gooey mud.

My daydreaming was interrupted by a mother scolding her child for spilling his apple juice and throwing a tantrum in the reference section of the library. "Sorry" was all she blurted out as she tugged the toddler by the arm. Her son was sticking his tongue out at me as they left. I smiled and waved.

Interesting things were always happening in the library. Like the time I found the man face down snoring into a book, his fingers locked so tightly onto the Truman biography that I had to wait until he awakened before I could retrieve it. The numerous times I've caught couples of all ages making out in the back corner. The "blue light" district I called it. I never called the cops on them. I'd just toss them out.

I took off my glasses and reached under the library counter to grab a handful of Gritty Kitty Litter that Doodle enjoyed so much. I had learned that it soaked up spilled liquids very well. I carried the bits of crushed stone, my hands cupped out in front as I approached the apple juice darkened carpet. I dropped it evenly over the stain, creating a chalk-dust cloud as I clapped my hands together.

The library clock seemed to tick more slowly than ever until it finally was closing time. I escorted Snider and the remaining patrons out of the library. I locked the door on their heels. Snider was in the middle of one of his lectures about senior citizens being disrespected by the youth of today or something like that; I was elsewhere. I wasn't paying attention.

Blanche Daring

I decided to go see my mother, I call her "Blanche," to enlist her help in identifying the language on the ancient skin. After all, she had been married to my father and may even have loved him at some point. She might be able to tell me something. I walked to the house she owns with her long time boyfriend, Glenn Burke, with its hand-painted "Burke Real Estate" sign in the window next to the pane that's broken, missing an entire corner of glass. It had a sock stuffed into the opening to keep the summertime flies from entering. The front steps were falling down. The doorbell was nothing more than two live bare wires you had to touch together, sparking a chime that could wake the peaceful dead.

I had decided to show Blanche the skin, but not tell her what it might be since she and Glenn would suddenly pucker up. The last thing I wanted was for this frozen mackerel and her sneaky friend kissing my behind, looking for a handout. She loved my older brother Don, beloved sloth that he is, more than me but I was fine with it.

"Yes?" she said. She was standing in the doorway, her hands on her hips. It had been a few months since I'd seen her, which is a tough task in such a tiny town. She was beginning to wrinkle and her bleached blond hair was thinning. It was sad when chicks started losing their hair. I'm sure she was having trouble being sixty years old.

It was funny how sweet she was when my father died, until she realized there was no life insurance, just a small pittance to cover his burial. She refused to pitch in for his headstone so I had to take out a loan. I loved him and there was no way the man was going to lay in an unmarked grave. His life warranted a tombstone.

"I want you to look at this and tell me what you think." I pulled the folded skin out of the manila envelope and handed it to her. I had to turn my back to the summertime sun that was shining directly into my eyes over the treetops.

"This is written in Welsh. I recognize the writing but I can't read it."

"Well, I remember my father could."

"Actually, he couldn't, but I do know someone who could read this for you."

"Are they in Waterville?"

"No. Remsen. It's about an hour drive from here up to Remsen, but I can't go anywhere because my car has no gas."

"I'll pay to fill your tank. How soon do you think you can take me to this person?"

Blanche rolled her eyes and looked at her gold-plated watch, while tapping her foot on the crooked front step. "Glenn, I'll be gone for a couple of hours!" she yelled into the house. She grabbed her smokes and keys off the coffee table.

"Let's go." She waved me to her gray K car that was new twenty years ago.

I hated having to ask her for anything, but didn't know anyone that could decipher this and at least I'd put gas in her car so she'd be appeased. I didn't look forward to this two-hour road trip with Blanche.

She threw the stacks of loose newspapers and overdue bills into the landfill in the back seat. Her ashtray overflowed with crumpled, yellowed butts. Ashes were strewn all over the place. The front seat puffed like a stinkball when I sat down. The sun had baked the odor into the shredded red velvet seat that had pieces of duct tape all over to keep the orange foam from spilling out.

I took my black bowler off and ran my fingers through my hair.

I looked at the tag inside that had faded with age. The stitching was crooked and didn't match the exterior craftsmanship.

"Why do you wear that stupid thing?"

"Because."

"I don't know why your father wore that ridiculous hat. When I first met him, he wasn't such a flake. The more he got into that stupid Loomis Gang thing, the weirder he became. He came home with that bowler one day; never took it off. He made me wonder if he was a genuine mad hatter; clinging to it like it was a baby blanket. I never knew where he got that thing or why he suddenly wore it, and to the day he died he never did explain it. And people wondered why I divorced the man."

I just shrugged my shoulders and placed the bowler back on my head. When I was a little girl and my father would place it on me, it seemed huge. I never thought it would fit. Today, with my thick locks, I fill it just right. I've grown into it and love to emulate my hero.

"Boy you look ridiculous in that thing. How are you supposed to get a husband when you wear Naugahyde pants and that stupid hat? By the way, I have a great raised ranch over on River Street that's going for fifty-five. It would be a perfect starter home for a married couple. It's got three bedrooms and one and a half baths. The basement has a slight seepage problem and there's a few termites—but that's fixable. Do you want me to show it to you? Any prospective men out there for you to grab?"

"I don't know. I really don't care." I wanted to scream at her that I didn't need a man to make my life complete, especially if he were like Glenn, a skunk with a pea-brain. She couldn't resist talking about real estate. If there was any way to make a sale, even if it meant me shacking up with a beer-guzzling wife beater with a pot-belly and infected toenails, she'd attempt it. Blanche would steal the coins off my dead eyes without regret. I wouldn't even be cold in the ground and she'd be jingling the coins in her pocket. In fact, she'd insist it was an entitlement of some sort.

There was no air conditioning in her car and the smoke billowing out of her nose made me gag. I opened the window all the way because the summer sun had warmed this tin can of a car so you couldn't even touch the cracked burgundy dashboard without burning your hand. I put my mouth to the cool flow of fresh air, like the family dog, inhaling with joy.

"You mind shutting that? My hay fever is acting up," barked Blanche, blowing a cloud of smoke in my direction.

I was grinding my teeth on my unlit cigarillo when she pulled into the one pump Quick Mart in Deansboro.

"Fill it up."

I was glad to be away from her for a minute while I pumped fourteen dollars and thirty-three cents into the tank. I went into the store and the overexcited screen door spanked me on my leather pant-behind before I could get in. There was a single cooler that I grabbed a diet lemon Snapple out of. I set the sweating glass bottle on the plywood counter. There were bins with raw fruits and vegetables that must've come from a backyard garden. A chubby red-haired teen with Opie-like freckles and bags under his eyes huffed at having to stop playing his GameBoy to wait on me.

"That it?"

"I have the gas out front too," I answered. I fished in my pocket to bring out a crumpled twenty-dollar bill. I hadn't a purse so I carried what cash I needed in my front pocket. I was talking through my nose because the store had an uncommonly strong onion smell.

I went back outside and snapped the top off my Snapple. I threw the cap in the fifty-five gallon drum that had half eaten candy in it, dispersing the swarm of flies and honeybees swirling around the mouth of the dented green receptacle. I got back into Blanche's car and was livid. She had done it. She had opened the manila envelope and was looking at the skin.

I felt violated. I blurted out, "What are you doing?"

"What?"

"Why are you looking at that?"

"I'm just interested. I can't read it or anything. You shouldn't be so bitchy. After all, I'm taking time out of my busy schedule to help you."

"Just forget it," I said. I took it back and tossed it into the envelope. I tucked it under my butt cheek, taking a fresh cigarillo out of the pack, pinching it between my lips and clenching my teeth down upon the sweet tobacco. "Where are we going anyway?" Hopefully, someplace where I could wrap my fingers around her throat and squeeze the color out of her.

"I told you, I know someone in Remsen who'll interpret this. See that gas station? I would never buy it. It's so old the gasoline has probably leaked into the groundwater. The next owner would have to have the dirt dug up and hauled away at a great expense. I wouldn't touch this cesspool with a flagpole."

"Imagine that," I mumbled, under my breath. That was a first.

I looked out the window as we left Deansboro behind. I was playing with the hardened, cracked molding around the edge of the window, testing its memory to my finger poking into it, trying hard not to look at Blanche, and wishing I had a job that paid enough to get my own vehicle.

Blanche pulled into Gilligan's Island Drive Thru outside of Clinton and ordered a "Lovey Deluxe combo meal," which included a triple-decker Skipper burger with all the fixings except pickles, which she loathed, spicy Ginger French fries, and a jug of Professor diet cola with no ice. She claimed they filled the cup with ice to rip you off, and load their pocketbooks. To her, soda was the big moneymaker. "It's nothing but caramel colored seltzer water," she'd always say. I didn't need to hear that for the ten-thousandth time.

She drove me crazy with her know-it-all personality. No matter the topic, she'd have the answer. No matter the question, she had a solution. For god's sake, the answer to every question in life couldn't be found in Vogue or TV Guide.

She didn't say anything when she pulled up to the drive-through window, just held out her palm for me to place a fin in it, in order to pass it along to the metal-mouthed teenager with the starched paper hat.

She didn't even say "thank you," instead, blurted out,

"Your father was a weird man."

Chapter 2

Ofnadwy Madarchen

I hoped this bizarre road trip with Blanche would be over soon. I was tiring of listening to her complain about my father. I put my father on a pedestal, above other humans. He was a martyr to the war of Blanche, a victim with a heart of glass, and the touch of a god.

After all, her main interest in life was to drink martinis in plastic champagne cups. She preferred shriveled olives and nuclear charged vodka, on sale because of its Chernobyl glow, to fine wine. Her only hobby was to bake her skin to crispy brown under UV tubes, then rub dollar store lotion over her basset hound neck.

"Your father had skinny calves, stringy hair, a fear of heights, snored like a bear, and an unhealthy obsession with a gang of thugs."

She did save the best for last, telling me, "I'm not sure he's your real father anyway."

I knew that was a lie because I've been told by more than a few people that I looked just like him. Besides, I couldn't stand the thought of being like her.

I heard this the entire way to the town of Remsen, on the edge of the Adirondack Park. We drove down the single dirt road that had a lonesome gas station/diner/bait shop/smoke house. It was constructed from wide slabs of gray pine boards and had a large, crude rendering of the Welsh flag, with its green and white striped background and a large red dragon breathing fire. Scrawled on a piece of cardboard in the store window was a selection of jerky: elk, deer, opossum, buffalo, squirrel, chipmunk, moose, and last but not least, rabbit.

"This shack has potential. Remsen is a beautiful town. The location is excellent for tourists heading up the Appalachian Trail. You'd just have to lure them off route 12. I'd say you could get this place for twelve five, tops." Blanche calculated. "Go on in there and get me a quarter pound of Bambi, would ya."

As I was getting out of the car, she was lighting another smoke. A man in a too-bright yellow tank top, whose hair had migrated from his scarred bald dome down to his shoulders and neck, waited on me. He handed me the blackened rope of meat that smelled like roasted skunk. There was a strip of amber flypaper hanging right above the meat that overflowed with dead flies. A fresh victim was stuck, flailing its little black legs, buzzing for its life.

"I put an extra piece in there for ya honey," he said. He smiled his blackened teeth at me, bouncing his eyebrows up and down like he was Jack Nicholson.

I tossed the bag of blackened meat to Blanche and she started right in with the inquisition.

"What is this tension that I'm noticing?"

I tried to keep my answer as short as possible. "Nothing," I mumbled, as I shut the door, trying not to look at her, as I adjusted my seatbelt.

"You have some sort of problem with me?"

"No."

"We're close to Ofnadwy's place. Your father asked me to connect him with her many years ago and Remsen is known as the area for Cymru, the people of Wales. I know because I grew up there. Keep that a secret will you?" She patted my knee. "It's pretty and all, but I don't want people to know I grew up in such a small place. Thanks."

We headed down a dirt road that had foot tall weeds growing in the center and Sumacs growing on the edges, leaning inward as if they were going to snatch us up off the ground, or swallow us up. After a few miles the trees cleared, revealing an open field with a little shack nestled in the middle. There was a small path leading to the front door. Parked in front was a rusty '57 pink Chevy with no windshield.

The weirdest thing was the wooden sign hanging from an old aluminum clothesline tree with something painted on it in red. As I got closer I realized that it was an actual outline of someone's hand with "heibio i" written on it with the name, Ofnadwy Madarchen. Was this woman a psychic? A fortune-teller? A witch?

I clutched the skin to my chest. The hair on the back of my neck rose at the sight of this fairy tale-like shack with its driftwood strips, it's crooked porch, and the fireplace that was made of boulders and mud. There was a hint of smoke breathing out of it. It was hotter than molten metal outside, and this person had a fire going?

The cottage had vines growing up the sides and fuzzy moss growing on the roof. A chipmunk sitting on its hind legs looked down at me quizzically then scrambled into a hole it had burrowed. There was a humming noise coming from the old Chevy. At first, I thought it was the engine running but from this angle I could see a throbbing bees nest hanging just above the steering wheel.

I noticed an outhouse off to the left that had a path worn into the dirt and a well on the other side that also had no grass growing around it. The rest of the yard was a wheat field overgrown with three-foot tall weeds.

"Just stay with me," ordered Blanche.

She picked up a large metal spoon off the porch railing and hit the large hanging cowbell.

"Claaang."

The front door opened a crack so Blanche pushed it the rest of the way, with me right on her heels, wincing at the squealing hinges. It was damp and musty and pitch black at first. As my eyes adjusted, I realized the windows were coated with dirt, the only light being the streaks that peaked in through the cracks in the walls and floor.

Ofnadwy seemed to appear out of nowhere. She lit a solitary candle which was sitting in a wine bottle on a makeshift table. She had stripes of light across her face from the gaps in her shack.

"Hiya, Blanche," she said.

"Hiya, Ofnadwy."

The old woman waved us over to sit on a plank balanced between two milk crates. I saw she was an albino, her pink eyes eerily reflecting the candle flame. Her thin blue veins bulged beneath her pure white skin. She reached out and touched my hands. Her fingers were covered with warts and her palms were clammy and cold like the rest of the cabin.

"Hiya, Daisy."

"How'd do you know my name?"

"I never forget du eyes," she said. She let go of my hands and pointed her skeletal white finger at my left eye. "You much "llai" when father bring you here. You have the hat... the bowler."

"I don't remember this place and I don't remember you." I took the hat off and scratched my scalp.

Blanche interrupted. "Yes, your father came here with you a long time ago with something like that skin you have. It had Welsh writing on it. I want to go outside and have a ciggy. Do you mind?"

As Blanche walked back out into the sunlight, dialing her cell phone, I could only wonder what my father had brought here and why he never told me about it.

Ofnadwy took the skin in both her hands and began telling me its secrets, writing down the English translation next to the Welsh letters. She couldn't give me the final location, but, instead, had given me what I needed to figure it out myself.

When she was done she held out her palms and my blank expression let her know to explain.

"Stipend."

Oh, crap, I had spent most of my cash.

"Can I mail you a payment?" I asked.

"No. No. I want a piece of you," she snarled. She pointed at my gold hooped nose piercing, which I couldn't give up because it was too new and the hole wasn't cauterized yet. I stood up and unzipped my leather pants, pulling them down past my hips. I bent over and unhooked the hoop from my belly button, placing it in her shaking white hands.

She laughed in a voice I could only describe as bone-rattling, that made the hair on my arms spike. Her pink eyes moistened from her joy as she got up and came around the table. She picked up my hand and patted it.

"Good girl," she said.

Daisy Daring

I had Blanche drop me off in front of the library. Not once did she ask me what Ofnadwy told me or wrote down. I took the skin to my

14

one room apartment that's attached to the rear of the building. I was excited for I soon would know the location of the gold. I decided to memorize it and would reveal it to nobody.

My salary was a measly thirteen thousand dollars a year, but I did get the tiny apartment along with utilities—my only bill was food. I didn't have any children to support, and at close to thirty, I doubted I'd have any now.

I figured my one and only chance at a normal life, and a family, evaporated back in my college days when I dumped Napoleoni for cheating on me. I don't know why I didn't stay in Halifax after finishing my Masters at Dalhousie University and get a better job, instead of returning to Blanche and upstate New York. Halifax was a wonderful international city with diverse cultures. Waterville was a quaint small town, but I had lived there my whole life and wanted something new.

Napoleoni was a handsome French-Canadian who used to give me goose bumps on my arms when he'd speak in his thick French accent and kiss my hand.

Staying in Halifax was my last chance to never have to deal with my selfish mother and my loser brother. I never got over my father dying while I was away. His story of the Oak Island's deadly water maze was what attracted me to Halifax in the first place. His tales compelled me to take a pilgrimage to Oak Island. When I discovered that it wasn't open to the public, Napoleoni pulled some strings and got us a private tour.

I remembered how we took a boat that he borrowed from a friend out to the island and then walked through the caverns, but we didn't venture too far for it was too dangerous. I couldn't believe anyone would want riches bad enough to delve any further into these caverns. The noise of the waves crashing into the hollow labyrinth of tubes emitted high pitched sounds that gave me an earache. It was maddening.

We had a picnic lunch on a blanket on a large flat rock watching the sea foam explode below us. We made love on the beach under the stars with no one else on the entire island.

When I told my father about my trip to Oak Island he was practically jumping through the phone with excitement. Napoleoni promised we could get him up here to see it for himself. My father never lived to see the island.

My father was my best friend and biggest supporter of my education. I was the first Daring besides him to go to college and he was very proud of me. My mother had divorced him when I was a young girl—about sixteen. She left me with him so she could have what she considered to be a jet-set lifestyle with Glenn Burke, the real estate mogul of Waterville. Blanche would scamp around town in her ten-dollar business suits trying to buy and sell houses, harassing family, friends, and strangers alike.

My father was the one with the passion for the Loomis Gang, teaching me the entire workings of their criminal activities that I found fascinating as a young girl. I'd sit at his feet with my legs crossed, my chin planted in my hands and my eyes wide with wonderment, while my brother Don would be out scamming kids out of their lunch money. All the while Blanche would roll her eyes and scoff at my father's interest in a bunch of "losers" as she called them. Little did she know the Loomis family came from New England aristocracy and were highly educated, this family of counterfeiters, thieves, arsonists, and murderers.

My father fascinated me with his tales of Wash and his stories of the stolen gold. How it'd be worth millions of dollars today. He dazzled me with tales of how the gold had long ago disappeared and rumor was that it was resting somewhere in Nine Mile Swamp. It made me yearn for the discovery that would finally allow me to live my dream of having my own private library named after my beloved—Doodle.

Chapter 3

Ben the Leisure Suit Man

"Ben the Leisure Suit Man" was the name I had given one older patron of the Waterville Public Library. He smelled like Ben Gay and wore this light blue polyester leisure suit from the seventies that was at least one size too small, and exposed his black dress socks. He flirted with any and all the women in the library. I think he thought he was suave. I actually did think he was kind of cute for an old man.

He always tried to mooch Charms blow pops from me. I had a soft spot for the children who came into the library, so I kept a supply of lollipops behind the counter, and I handed them out to the children wide-eyed and ready to discover the world in books. I was proud of any child that would shut off the television and back away from a video game to come to the library. I wanted to lure them in to read and reward them with sweet treats. I didn't mind scraping the gum out from under the tables and seats with a putty knife after everyone left. I'd always give Ben the Leisure Suit Man a blow pop and he loved me for it.

Daisy Daring

I had spread my father's old notes across the kitchen table and laid the notes from Ofnadwy next to them.

Doodle was eating his tuna Meow Mix not caring what I was doing, flapping his stub of a tail across some of the wrinkled note

17

paper. I poured myself a goblet of Tug Boat Red in my favorite pewter mug. I loved the blood red wine from Lucas Vineyards.

My father had been a friend of George Walter, who was the biographer of Wash and company, and who had written a book titled "The Loomis Gang." It was obvious that Shane didn't know the Welsh language or he wouldn't have sought me out.

I was amazed that the "code," as my father called it, was really nothing more than Welsh. All I had to do was decipher it using the Welsh alphabet provided to me by Ofnadwy Madarchen. I wasn't sure if Wash Loomis was Welsh or if he learned the language from some of his gang members that came from the Welsh town of Remsen.

"Doodle, here sweetie. C'mon puss, puss." I held out a nubbin of sardine I had just cut, causing the old tabby to jump onto my lap and chomp on the oily treat. He went back to the floor and licked his chops while purring. I took my cowboy boots off and rubbed my bare feet, trying to soften my corns. Billy Jack never wore socks under his cowboy boots, so I decided not to as well, but my aging arches ached.

After several hours, I had only transcribed a little of the document, so I walked to my apartment, smoking a cigarillo. I was thinking about what I'd do with my share of the loot, if it were indeed a map to the hidden Loomis fortune on the skin. I remembered my father telling me about a map that he had seen that may reveal the treasure and this might be the one he was referring to. Perhaps Ofnadwy had seen it when my father was up there.

I was frustrated in my attempt to translate the gibberish at the bottom that at first appeared to be Welsh but now I wasn't sure. There was something missing. The letters seemed different to me.

I put on my Kevlar gloves and took out my whittling knife and started slicing thin layers of basswood away from the newest member of my Noah's Ark—an elephant. My father had taught me to whittle. He had completed many animals for the ark, leaving me to carve their mates. I still had a ways to go but I did have pairs of tigers, lions, giraffes, camels, and a few more.

Carving detailed animals from an eight-inch by eight-inch by three-inch block of soft wood was much tougher than it looked. It usually took me about six months just to complete one animal. The knife was dull so I sat at the grinding wheel and pumped the foot pedal making the stone wheel go round, placing the edge of the blade against it, flipping it over to even out the sharpening on the other side. Sparks bounded off my leather pants and hissed before hitting the floor.

I was tired but I wanted to finish the elephant before going to bed. So I finished the carving and was quite pleased with my efforts. Maybe some day, I'll be as accomplished as my father was. I scrubbed Jumbo with a vegetable brush and soap before I rubbed rabbit skin glue all over it to seal the cracks. Then I placed it next to the kitchen sink to dry. It wouldn't go up on the shelf with the other creatures of God until I was finished.

The hobby break cleared my mind and helped me think about what I would do with the gold. The Doodle Library was what I'd do. With my own library I could keep out all the disrespectful people who ripped pages out of periodicals, brought books back with their children's chocolate handprints on them, and trampled dirt on the rugs. I would only allow those people that I liked to take books out or sit in my reading room, making it a sanctuary for serious minded people to segregate themselves from the uninformed.

I blew a large puff of smoke out the screened window of my kitchen and laughed at the scattering insects who had been trying to push their way into the lighted room. No science fiction in the Doodle Library. I resented having to carry a genre that I considered foolish, vowing to myself there will be no such ilk in my library, instead it shall be stocked only with topics I like. My own banned books. They can burn all science fiction for all I cared.

I went back to my attempt to decipher the animal skin and ran into a stone wall. I knew Wash was too clever to make his directions too easy to crack. I spent the rest of the night tapping my burning cigar ashes into my large green depression glass ashtray, deciding that if I ever broke the code, I would never reveal what I knew until I had to. I didn't want to go back to Ofnadwy unless it was the last resort.

I've never been the kind of person that sneaks around, but this was my best chance to get out of my meager paying job that everyone in town thinks is so easy. They claim I'm overpaid. Even the mayor thinks he can come in and hit on me declaring I'm his property

19

because the town pays me. I would love to tell his wife about our long ago affair, although I have a feeling she already knows. I have to admit he does a great job of running the town, but he has a nasty personality. I want to forget about him. Just because I have no man in my life, doesn't mean I'm interested in any man who comes along—even if he's the mayor. When I find a new Napoleoni, I'll move on love.

I finally fell asleep around three in the morning. I was pumped about the possibility of the riches. I had gold fever insomnia. I kept rehearsing what I'd say to Shane to be sure he didn't take the skin away. And yet the skin may reveal absolutely nothing at all, knowing the reputation of Wash Loomis.

Shane Loomis

I was startled awake by a pounding on my back door. Doodle scrambled off my feet and hid under my bed. I sat up and rubbed the glue from my sleepy eyes, and pulled my pants back on. My head pounded with a Tug Boat Red hangover. It was early. Six in the morning and the June heat was already beginning to heat up my non-air conditioned apartment. I shuffled to the backdoor to find Shane Loomis and his girlfriend.

As I opened the door, they pushed their way in, wearing the same clothes as yesterday. They were grumbling under their breath as they sat at my kitchen table. I poured myself a cup of my home-brewed, iced green tea, and dropped in a wedge of lemon and a spoonful of clove honey. Shane was looking at the skin with rapt attention. I knew he'd never figure it out because Welsh was a dead language that few spoke.

"How did you find this anyway?" I asked. I sat in the empty chair, tapping my finger on the yellowed skin.

"I was bouncing a tennis ball in my trailer against the portrait of my great-great grandparents when it fell off the wall and smashed revealing this," replied Shane, shaking the skin at me. "You going to tell me what this means?"

"I thought the Loomis family lost everything when Sheriff Filkins and the vigilantes burned their house to the ground?" I was interested in how this portrait survived because just as quickly as the Loomis women were bringing their belongings out of the burning house, the posse threw the stuff back in, leaving the Loomis brood with nothing but the clothes on their backs.

"Beats me. All's I know is that it somehow ended up in my trailer. Maybe my old man left it there, who knows?" said Shane.

"The text is written in a language that I've been unable to decipher. But give me a little more time and I'll crack the code."

"I thought you were smart? I'm not so sure you didn't already break it and you're not tellin'."

"I'm not sure what it says. Honestly!"

"All right, all right, I believe you. But when you find out what it says, remember, it's my family fortune, and you'd better tell me where it is."

"Shane, I want to strike a deal with you. If I discover this is the key to the hidden loot, we split the gold fifty-fifty," I suggested, holding out my hand to shake.

"You whore!" yelled Jessica, as she backhanded me. I fell out of my chair and could feel the blood welling up in my nose. I pinched it shut but it was too late because a stream of red liquid had run over my lips and dripped off my chin onto the floor. My glasses had flown off and I swiped my free hand back and forth across the floor until I found them and put them back on. They were bent.

"Jessica, calm down!" yelled Shane, as he held her back. She had my whittling knife in her hand and was trying to get past Shane.

"I say we torture her for the information. Maybe she has it written down here somewhere," she screamed, and threw the papers on my table to the floor.

Shane was able to get the knife away from her and set her down in the chair. He put his arm around me and helped me back up. I said nothing while he wet a paper towel in the sink and wiped my chin. I could feel the tears welling up in my eyes and I fought hard not to let them flow while Jessica stared at me with hatred in her eyes.

"I will take sixty percent and give you forty percent," offered Shane. "That's the best I can do and it's more than fair." He held my hands in his and I was hypnotized by his deep blue eyes. "Now you figure out what this thing says and it better not be something stupid. I know it must be a map because my mother told me when she was alive that her great-great-grandfather had written down where he hid the treasure. Just tell me where we find the gold."

"It's not that simple."

Chapter 4

Cornelia Loomis: The Loomis Gang 1864

Cornelia Loomis wasn't called "Outlaw Queen" for nothing and she was going to give her sisters Lucia and Charlotte a lesson she had long perfected while attending a fancy party of the Clinton, NY elite. The soirée was held at the Hamilton House, the mansion of Alexander Hamilton, in the fall of 1860.

The Loomis Gang excelled in counterfeiting. A perfect replication of the invitations to the ball was completed by Denio Loomis with minimum effort. When the Loomis women arrived at the mansion, the Remington family, the current owners of the house, went to the back room and discussed the fact that the Loomis women were not on the invitation list but to deny them admittance was sure to bring the wrath of the gang. They decided to let them in but asked Palmer, their butler, to keep his eyes focused on the ladies and not allow them to wander into the expansive rooms that held treasures they might plunder.

The party was being held to show off Ann Marie Remington to the potential suitors in attendance. She was a loathsome creature, round as she was tall, whose corset strings groaned to keep her from further expansion. She had a fever as a young child that claimed her teeth so she carried a fan that she held up to her mouth when she flirted. The men in attendance were more entranced by the family fortune of the Remington's than by Ann Marie. By contrast, the striking Loomis ladies caused the usual hen cackling and mustache stroking that only Venus replications can inspire.

The well-educated Loomis girls were taught their skills by their

23

parents and brothers. Being academically schooled was a rarity amongst middle nineteenth century American women.

Cornelia and her sisters wore their best floor length dresses and blended in among the rich and powerful of the Mohawk Valley. The men lined up to kiss their hands and smile at their batting eyelashes. The men were the leaders of the valley, politicians, lawyers, and professors from the local Hamilton College. Most certainly they were easy pickings for the Loomis ladies.

There was a string orchestra in the foyer playing furiously while servants walked the party with platters of food and goblets of champagne.

Cornelia felt the breath of Palmer on the back of her neck and with a knowing wink the three sisters split up. Cornelia watched her little sister, Charlotte move in on an unsuspecting gentleman.

"Good evening," said the man.

"Good evening," responded Charlotte, eyelashes fluttering.

"I'd like to introduce myself. I'm Ezekiel Smith, Esq."

"Charlotte Loomis." She held out her gloved hand and the bald old man with the waxed handlebar mustache pecked his lips causing her to snicker and blush.

"Enchanted, my dear," replied Smith.

"I'm the counselor to the Remington family and many others in attendance here."

Charlotte nodded her head and smiled. Her teeth were straight, white, and mesmerizing.

"I live in the Stanley house up on Ridgeway hill. It's very lonely up there."

"Oh, I'm sorry, are you…"

"No, I'm not widowed, but my wife and my three intolerable children make me wish I were." He pulled a solid gold watch out of his vest pocket and snapped it open. "The time is short and I must be departing." He put the watch back into his pocket.

Cornelia had positioned herself so that she had Palmer facing her and she could watch her little sister pick the pocket of the bald man she was flirting with. Smith kissed Charlotte's hand and Cornelia snickered at the quick hands her little sister employed while removing the watch.

"Are we ready to go yet?" asked Charlotte, the youngest and least experienced of the Loomis girls. She had beads of sweat running down her forehead.

"Shhh—quiet," whispered Cornelia, as she grabbed her little sister by the elbow and pushed her to the door. "Just smile and look straight ahead." Lucia was bringing up the rear in case she had to distract any of the curious.

Ann Marie Remington suddenly cut in front of them. She had several other debutantes behind her and she nodded to Palmer who quickly shut the door with his white gloved hands.

"Our fur muffs are missing and I know you stole them Cornelia," she said, pointing her finger at Cornelia's face.

"I have no idea what you're referring too." She placed her opened hand against her bosom.

"Into the back room!" Ann Marie demanded, pushing the Loomis brood ahead of her. The musicians stopped playing and the chattering voices suddenly fell silent. They shut the door behind them and turned up the oil lamp to brighten the bedroom. "Give them back and we won't call for the constable." Ann Marie knew the Loomis reputation for arson. Wash and Grove were certain to return and burn the mansion to the ground if the Loomis ladies were harmed in any way.

"No reason to be rude. Show a little decorum," reprimanded Cornelia, doing all the talking as her sisters fell in behind her arms that were spread out like butterfly wings.

Ann Marie pushed Cornelia to the armchair and pulled up her skirt, revealing fur muffs stacked on both of her legs, all the way up to her thighs. Ann Marie and the others clawed them off, getting no protest from the Loomis ladies. Cornelia knew she was caught and would just steal them some other time.

"Now get out and never come back!" screamed Ann Marie, as she clutched her brown mink muff.

"I think you're a barbarous person," said Cornelia. She straightened her dress and tucked loose strands of brown hair back into her bun. The sisters marched out single file, never to return to another Mohawk Valley social event.

Five days later, Hamilton House was burned to the ground. The Loomis gang was rumored to be in Clinton at the time, but was never charged for the crime.

Chapter 5

Shane Loomis

"I don't have the information up here to solve this," I said, tapping my temple with my pointer finger. My nose had stopped bleeding, but my head still throbbed from the blow. My out-of-whack-glasses didn't sit right on my nose. "I'll keep my word that you'll know as soon as I decipher this. I've lived here all my life and have heard all kinds of rumors about stolen gold hidden in Nine Mile Swamp. Are you saying its true? The Loomis' treasure really is hidden somewhere in the swamp?"

"Hell, everyone knows there's gold in the swamp and many have died searching for it." replied Shane, looking at the skin upside down. It was about two feet by two feet when spread out, and was covered in extremely small Welsh calligraphy.

"You'll have to leave it with me a little longer until I can figure it out." It was hard to talk with Jessica smoking, snapping her nails together, and mumbling under her breath the whole time. Ofnadwy had helped me, but I'd have to crack the rest of it myself.

"I still live on the same hill where the Loomis house stood. My trailer is only a hundred feet from where they burned the house and hung Grove. I want to buy the piece of the tree they hung him from that's on display in the historical building. This fortune will put the Loomis Gang back on the map. I bet I can get my book published too," Shane boasted. He took out his comb and ran it through his hair that had fallen over his forehead.

"You're a writer?" I asked, not so shocked since in their heyday, the Loomis family was a very smart bunch. That's what separated them from Jesse James and Butch Cassidy—brains.

"He's not very good. His book was rejected by everyone," announced Jessica, rolling her eyes.

"What's it about?"

"It's about my heritage, about the activities of the Loomis Gang. I can't understand why my family has been forgotten by history. The Gang controlled most of upstate New York from Canada to Pennsylvania and from the Finger Lakes to Vermont," he said passionately while waving his hand in the air. "With over two hundred members, they were the largest American family crime syndicate in the nineteenth century."

"I would love to look at your manuscript sometime." I was curious to see it. There was more to Shane than met the eye. "Well, you'll have to leave this skin with me. We have to make a pact not to discuss this with anyone."

"Why do you look at me when you say that?" snarled Jessica. "You figure this out or I'll kill you. I'll smack you again." She raised her hand, causing me to cover my nose and duck under the table like a beaten hound dog.

"If this is going to work you're going to have to mellow out," said Shane. He grabbed Jessica and walked her out the door. "We'll be back tomorrow."

They left with me on my knees in my kitchen. I looked around my tiny apartment, thinking if this was indeed a map, and if the legend of the hidden gold was true, I wouldn't have to live here anymore. Doodle came from out of the shadow and sat next to me, lapping up a droplet of my blood.

I took out my gray paint and dripped a little into a metal cup, dropped in a little Arabic gum and a pinch of ox gall powder and mixed. These secret ingredients keep the colors from running into one another; however Jumbo was going to be all gray, I mixed the concoction out of habit. After I painted the entire elephant, I placed a small metal pan on the stove and dropped a hunk of beeswax in, melting it slowly. Once the wax was liquefied, I removed the pan from the stove and mixed in some turpentine. You never put the turpentine in while the wax was on the stove, unless you wanted a fire. I coated the entire elephant with the wax to seal him and shine him for the forty-day and forty-night journey and placed him on my kitchen table. Once he was dry, I'd introduce him to his life-mate on the shelf.

I looked up at the clock and realized I was going to be late opening the library. It was the middle of July and some kid and his parent were always waiting for the door to open. And with my luck it'd be the mayor's wife and son. The little boy always had shiny new clothes, the best fashions of the day. The wife seemed jealous of me, perhaps she knew about her husband and me.

I jumped into the shower then quickly got dressed.

When I walked into the library from my attached apartment, my hair was still wet, and I could see someone was at the door. They started pounding, but I couldn't see who it was as my glasses were fogged and the strong morning sun was shining in my face. I opened the door and Snider walked in looking rather nervous. He was staring at my swollen nose.

"Good morning," he mumbled and walked past me carrying the *Crabtree Courier*. It had been on the front stoop rolled with a rubber band around it, and now was tucked under his arm. He had on his green work pants with the oil stains on the rear, and the ever present odors of gasoline and grass clippings. He was a landscaper by trade and spent the rest of his free hours here with Doodle and me.

The phone was ringing so I jumped around the counter.

"Hello. Waterville Public Library."

"Yes. I'm looking for a pirate's dream. A sunken chest."

"So you're looking for a sunken chest?"

The boys on the other end were laughing again and I just slammed the phone down since I was too tired to play around. When I get the Doodle library, phones will be banned—all of them, cell and land lines. Damn curse of Edison.

Chapter 6

Harry Daring

I remembered the time when I was five years old and my father took me to Bouckville for the annual antique show. He bought me a little cast iron horse and rider, along with a few cowboys that were missing arms and legs. We went back to our apartment and played with them on the floor. The summer was my favorite time because he was off from teaching at Waterville High where he was the history instructor. The other teachers worked other jobs in the summer, but my father never did anything but play with me and try to teach Don and me all kinds of cool stuff.

"Here comes the Loomis Gang," he'd say, pretending to fire his little metal pistol, taking off his bowler hat and rapping on it to simulate horse hooves. He'd wear a blue handkerchief covering his mouth like the bandits of old.

"I'm the sheriff in these parts and you're going to the hoosegow," I'd answer.

"You'll never catch me Filkins," he'd continue, hiding one of the cowboys and the horse in his bowler, then placing it over his heart. "Wash has disappeared into Nine Mile Swamp. You dare not follow." He smiled, knowing he had me.

"Darn! You haven't seen the last of me," I warned, galloping my miniature iron man into the sunset while my father tapped his fingers on the bowler simulating the hoof beats of the escaping animal.

"Honestly, Harry," complained Blanche, who stood over us with her hands on her hips, tapping her foot on the wooden floor of our apartment. "All the other teachers work in the summer, and this is how you spend your days?"

"I'm just teaching Daisy a lesson on the Loomis Gang." He removed the bandana, wiped his brow with it, and put his bowler back on. My mother looked at me with disgust as she took a deep drag on her unfiltered cigarette, exhaling a toxic cloud down upon us. She hated the name my father had picked out for me. Having chosen the name for my older brother, she had bequest the naming rights of her daughter to her husband. I loved being named Daisy Alice Daring for my monogram spelled DAD. I remembered Blanche saying it was ridiculous of my father to name me so queerly.

She lit another cigarette, using the current one as the starting device and blew another puff down at us, making me cough, as she stomped away in her new high heels.

Shane Loomis

I was at my desk that afternoon stamping in the returned books that had been left in the box out front. Shane came walking in by himself carrying a manuscript under his arm. He set it down in front of me and took out his comb and cleared his black mop of hair from his brow.

"Hi," he said.

"Hello."

"I got my book here I'd like you to look at for me. I've spent three years writing this when I wasn't mopping the floor over to the Food King." He placed the box down and opened the flap. I liked the title, *The Greatest Gang on Earth*. I was relieved his hotheaded girl-friend wasn't with him. The manuscript was handwritten on a yellow legal pad; the pages were unnumbered and there were a lot of crossed out lines and notes in the margins. This was sure to be as ugly as it looked.

"I would be delighted to critique it for you."

"I got to tell you, I'm really excited about the possibility of finding my family fortune. I'll be able to stay home and write all day."

I have to say that I was impressed, seeing that most young men in our area would rather splurge on a truck, a four-wheeler, a snowmobile, and other kinds of adolescent toys. I still had to be cautious. I could never forget he was a Loomis and I had a feeling he was playing good cop/bad cop with his girlfriend as a ploy to trick me.

I couldn't resist gushing. "I'm hoping to decipher the code for you soon. I'm making progress. I hope Jessica will act a little more mature." I pushed my crooked glasses back up my nose, took off my bowler and set it on the counter.

"Don't you worry, I had a talk with her and she's on board. You'll get no more trouble from her, and she promised she'll keep her mouth shut. She wants to get married as soon as we find the gold. I'm not so sure about that, but I'm the last of the Loomis and maybe it should be that way. Boy I'd like to get my book made into a movie. I'd love to get Cruise or Penn in the lead role."

He picked up the bowler and fiddled with it, almost placing it on his head. He set it back down on the counter. Doodle had appeared and was rubbing himself against Shane's legs.

"We all have to remember to keep quiet about this," I warned. "You know the fever people have long had for the lost treasure of the Loomis Gang."

"Well I can guarantee that Jessica won't talk but I did already kind of mention it to Lyndon Johnson."

"The reporter? Are you nuts? How the hell are we supposed to get this done when everyone in town will know about it? As far as we know that old skin has nothing but gibberish on it and you're telling a reporter we have the location of the treasure?"

I was really pissed because, even if we happened to discover the truth and get the money, a two-way split can become a ten-way pretty darn fast. Granted the *Crabtree Courier* was a small town newspaper without the circulation of the New York Times, but damage could be done to our mission for once something's in print it can end up anywhere.

"Don't worry. He always buys me a beer at the Spit Pea. He's a cool guy and besides he said he's got 'journalistic integrity,' or something like that."

"Shhh," I said, reaching around Shane to stamp a Harry Potter book that a young man was clutching like a new toy. I opened it to place the due slip into the back envelope and took out a Snickers candy bar wrapper some prankster had left in it.

I was always finding items in the books people went to check out: parking tickets, a Polaroid photo showing a farmer holding a chicken, coupons for the Food King, a used tea bag, grocery lists, a band-aid with Elmo on it, leaves from trees, usually Red Maple, phone bills, and a drivers license amongst other oddities. I kept all these in a box under the counter, but very few people ever came to my lost and found to claim their love letters and bills.

There was also a variety of odors emitting from the pages. I recognized chocolate, Aqua Velva, baby powder, garlic, cooking oil, and cigarette smoke among them. I handed the Harry Potter book back to the little boy. Shane and I resumed talking once the front bell stopped clinging.

"I still can't believe you haven't deciphered that writing yet. I figured you'd be able to since everyone knew your father was friends with George Walter," he said, smiling and bobbing his head. "Hell it looks like chicken scratch to me."

A customer was behind him waiting to ask me a question. "Can I help you?" I asked, looking around Shane at the young man with the skateboard under his arm.

"You got the internet yet?"

"No. I don't know when we'll ever have that here at the library." I didn't want illegal songs being downloaded on my watch. I didn't want the internet here. I loved the fact the library was all on cards, forcing the kids to learn the Dewey Decimal System. When I have my own library it will be the way it was when I was a child—no computers.

"This place is a dumb ass dump," complained the kid, waving his hand.

"Watch your language in front of the lady."

"Or what?" the kid said, pulling a black handle out of his pocket. He pressed the button and a switchblade appeared. The blade reflected the sunlight from the window into my eyes, forcing me to hold my hand up to block it.

Shane moved like a mongoose, grabbing the kid's wrist and turning it under until he dropped the knife, which fell and stuck in the floor. The kid was bent down almost to the floor himself.

"Oww, you're breaking my wrist!"

"Apologize to the lady."

"Shane don't," I screamed in horror.

"Shhh," he cautioned, looking at me, his black eyes intense, a large vein pulsated down his forehead. He twisted a little harder and I could hear ligaments snapping. The kid whimpered a sorry, as teardrops fell to the floor. "That's good manners. Now get the hell out of here." Shane let go of the kid's wrist and the injured boy slumped to the floor crying, while holding his injured paw. His fingers were frozen in a clawed position.

Shane then grabbed the kid by the shirt collar, walked him out of the door and kicked him in the butt. Then he threw the skateboard out after him. I was sure the kid's parents would ignore what happened when they heard it was a Loomis. Even though Wash and Grove had been dead a hundred years, people were still afraid to have their houses burned to the ground. The Loomis legacy cast a long shadow in Madison County.

"Being a Loomis sure has its advantages."

"Not really, Daisy," he picked up the switchblade and snapped it back into position and handed it to me. "Here's a present for you. Being a Loomis has no advantages. I walk down the street and people cross to the other side. The women clutch their purses and snicker to each other," he said, pausing to comb his hair. "I tried getting a better job than bagging groceries at the Food King but people are afraid I'll steal everything. Look, I have to go, but I'll be back tomorrow to see if you've made any more progress."

"Okay."

I watched him go out of the library and felt ashamed that I was starting to feel something for him. It was the same kind of fire in my heart that I felt when I met Napoleoni in college. I'm close to thirty and he's twenty but I still can't control my emotions. I flipped through the pages of his manuscript dreading the bad review I'd have to give him. Perhaps I could find something redeeming in this pile of crumpled paper.

I just couldn't understand what he saw in Jessica, the immature loud mouth. He needed a more mature woman, a woman that could nurture his creative side, a woman who could help him reach his potential.

A teenage patron set a live spider on my desk.

"Is this poisonous?"

"Get that out of here," I said. I quietly stepped away from the counter. The kid left with the black arachnid cupped in his hands. I swore the patrons got weirder the longer I sat behind the counter.

Once a patron asked me for a book by, "Reagan, first name 'President.'" Another time a patron said, "I want the book I took out before, you know, the blue one." The best was the middle aged professional student who asked me to write his dissertation since I had nothing better to do but stare off into space all day.

Daisy Daring

I played my Johnny Cash again, humming *A Boy Named Sue*, while drinking my Tug Boat Red, confident that I would never decipher this writing. I snipped the tip off of my last brown cigarillo with my chrome clippers. I clacked open my limited edition Elvis Zippo lighter that I bought in the parking lot of the Food King from some gypsies. They sold mostly to little old ladies seeking cheap presents that looked expensive for their husbands with the shorts and black socks.

I lit the cigar for a change, puffing on it until the tip glowed orange, hoping the nicotine buzz would spark a Prometheus moment, dreaming of the things I'd do with my riches as I exhaled a large toxic cloud that chased Doodle away. The money wouldn't just get me my library and my teeth fixed, but perhaps a return to Halifax.

I hadn't been to Dalhousie University since I graduated. Travel on my meager salary was limited to trips to the Adirondacks or the Poconos. A trip up to Boldt Castle on the St. Lawrence River was better than an expensive trip to a styrofoam theme park any day. I had to admit that the scenery of the Mohawk Valley was breathtaking, almost to the point where I took it for granted.

I wondered if Napoleoni still looked the same. Perhaps I could spruce myself up and search him out. After a last gulp of wine, I sliced a hunk of horseradish cheese and shook my head no, knowing I could never handle seeing him again. Doodle was the only man in my life now.

I took out a freshly cut block of basswood and drew lines with my black Sharpie. I had decided that my next animal would be a zebra. I took down the one my father had carved twenty years earlier and eyeballed the features while I drew the rough outline of my male zebra. I pushed the button on the switchblade and wondered if I could carve with it. The blade was long and thin and I doubted it would last long on my grinding wheel. I carefully snapped the blade back into the handle, took out my whittling knife and blocked out the large hunk of wood to get the rough carving of the animal. I started to carve the finer features until my hands began cramping. It had been getting tougher lately to carve for long periods. I set the knife and carving aside.

I walked into my small bathroom and turned my head from side to side looking at the crow's feet next to my eyes. As I pulled some strands of hair down to cover them, I realized I was getting a few gray hairs mixed in with my dark brown locks. I brushed my teeth with my hydrogen peroxide, baking soda whitener, bobbing my head to the last song on my disc, *The Essential Johnny Cash*.

I set the Wash Loomis skin to the side and picked up the manuscript box with the yellow pages. Shane's handwritten chicken scratch was a little tough to read. I took off my glasses and tried to bend them straight when one of the lenses popped out onto the floor. I had to get a small piece of scotch tape to hold it back into place, realizing I must look like a complete moron with these, but I couldn't afford a new pair. They still felt crooked when I placed them back on my nose; I guess they'll always be a little off, just like me.

Doodle had jumped up on the table and was nudging the papers with his nose, then lay down on a stack and purred. I had no clue how old my boy was but I knew he didn't have a heck of a lot of time left. He was slowing down and had much more gray than I. I started reading and with every sentence, every paragraph, my chin lowered further until it hit my chest.

Chapter 7

Cornelia Loomis: The Loomis Gang 1864

Cornelia strung two warmed potatoes and put them on the black horse, letting them hang down and bleach the color out of the neck like Grove and Wash had taught her. The Loomis Gang made their fortune stealing horses and changing their appearances, often reselling them back to the original owner. Cornelia paused to wipe the sweat from her brow. The August heat warmed Nine Mile Swamp, the humidity was as thick as tree tar.

Cornelia was excited about the latest batch of horses. Since the start of the Civil War the price they got for horses had risen considerably. They would place the horses on a barge set for New York City to sell them to Fredericka "Marm" Mandelbaum, who became a millionaire by fencing stolen goods to the Union. They shared their profits with Bill Alvorde, the captain of the boat called the "Dan Hartwell." It was a solid vessel that could hold a dozen horses and keep away from law enforcement all the way down the Erie Canal.

"That's looking perfect," complimented Wash, looking over her shoulder, rubbing the back of the horse.

"I'm almost finished," answered Cornelia, knowing the horse would be escorted deep into the swamp where nobody dared venture. She took off her hat to wipe the sweat from her brow. She had put on her "man" clothes. That's what gang member Big Bill Rockwell had called them. Cornelia wore slacks, for the chore of altering a horse wasn't meant to be done in a hoop dress and white linen gloves.

The Loomis Gang was rumored to have a hidden meadow sur-

39

rounded by swamp water somewhere. Its never been found. Grove had come up with the idea of hiding planks in the brush and, when needed, could construct a temporary bridge to cross the narrowest part of the swamp. They would leave the horses on the island until they had enough to fill a ferry on the Erie Canal. They would pay off Bill Alvorde and give him extra cash in case any constable encountered on the way to supplying horses for the Union had to be paid off.

"Wash, that's my horse God damn you!" complained Harold Williamson, as he walked up the knob to the back barn. Grove and Wash came out of the barn. Denio ran out of the house, while Charlotte and Lucia stayed on the porch to guard their mother, Rhoda.

George Washington Loomis, Sr. and Rhoda had taught their children the art of thievery, as well as schooled their brood in academics and etiquette. It was unheard of in America back in those days for any woman to be able to read. The Loomis women were well-read and as well educated as any man; they would be heard.

"We don't have your horse," insisted Wash, standing between Harold and the barn.

The man whistled and the horse returned with a loud neigh. "See-that? There's my Betsy Blue."

Wash then had Cornelia walk the horse out into the pasture. Cornelia had done a masterful job of clipping the mane and potato bleaching light-colored spots all over the black coat.

"As you can see Harold, this here's not your horse," said Cornelia, taking a carrot from her front pocket, holding it up to the horse's lips for him to munch.

Harold clapped his hands together and yelled "Up" while raising his arms to the sky like a rainmaker. The horse pulled free of Cornelia and lifted its fore legs off the ground, waving its hooves up and down before landing and snorting. Harold then lowered his hands to the ground and the horse bowed down and snorted into the dirt, sending up a small cloud of dust. "Now that's my Betsy Blue."

"Here's your horse," said Cornelia, handing the reins to Harold. Grove held the fence until Wash nodded him to the side. Harold said not a word of protest regarding the new look of his prized possession, realizing he was fortunate to get out of Loomis Knob with his horse and his life. He was a mile away before any Loomis spoke.

"Cornelia, what was that?" asked Grove, kicking the fence. "I worked real hard to get that horse."

"It was the correct gesture," she answered, brushing the remnants of hay off the front of her slacks.

"She's right Grove," said Wash.

"I say we steal it again and burn his damn barn to the ground," shouted Grove.

"He's too magnificent a beast to be shot to death," warned Cornelia, crossing her arms. Grove nodded his head reluctantly and went back to his chores, while their mother contentedly puffed on her pipe.

Chapter 8

Daisy Daring

It was close to noon and I was wondering where in the blazes Shane was. The cops never did come to arrest him for assaulting that kid. I thought it was barbaric, however, I did like the knight in shining armor maneuver. I had left the skin back in my apartment but had brought the rough draft of Shane's novel with me to the library.

His grammar was so bad I didn't know where to start. The misspelled words outnumbered the correct ones and the many annoying sentence fragments left me dizzy. But I was also stunned at the poetry of his words and the clever way the plot moved. The character development was excellent. I knew I never could write as well, regardless of my education. I always felt writing was a God-given talent, like singing, dancing, or painting. But for some reason, writers are seldom seen as serious artists. I dedicated my life to them, and their altar of words shall one day be represented in my private library.

Snider was in his usual place. I couldn't locate Doodle, who tended to hide more and more with the increasing number of children coming into the library during the summer vacation period. The children would be dropped off by their parents to roam unsupervised in the aisles of the library screaming, crying, and giggling at each other. I never imagined being a nanny when I was in college. I always viewed library science as a romantic art form not as a daycare facility. At least I might be able to make a difference and introduce the little ones to the world of books.

As the bell on the library door rang, I tried not to notice Lyndon Johnson coming towards me with his steno pad flipped open, clicking his pen in step with his dirty work boots. I always thought he looked rather odd wearing jeans and boots with his white dress shirt and the same loosened red paisley necktie. I wondered if the man owned any other clothing. He attempted to camouflage his balding head with a swirl of his whitening hair. A drop of shoe polish on his lip gave away his dyed black handlebar mustache.

"Good afternoon, Ms. Daring."

"Hello, Mr. Johnson, and how can I help you today?"

"Well, I had a discussion last night with Shane Loomis over a few beers at the Spit Pea, and was wondering if you'd like to elaborate on the little treasure hunt you're planning."

"I don't know what you're talking about." I tried not to look him in the eye while I walked around the counter and pushed the cart towards the fiction section to place the returns in their rightful place. "Please be quiet," I whispered, adjusting my glasses. He was right on my heels like a typical reporter, taking notes in his opened tablet. He was the one and only writer for the *Crabtree Courier*, but he acted like he was a hotshot Pulitzer Prize winner at *The New York Times*.

Waterville is a quaint little town with one flashing stoplight and no modern fast food restaurants, not the place for aspiring investigative reporters. I heard that Lyndon Johnson was once on his way to the big time as a crackerjack reporter for the *Albany Gazette*, but because of his drunkenness and mean temper, was fired and retreated to Waterville. So, like I, he thought he was too big for this little town. He, like I, had had to settle.

"I know Shane found some kind of map revealing the location of the lost gold of the Loomis Gang. He tells me it's Wash Loomis' stolen fortune. You know this is a huge story and I'll break it with or without you."

"I can't help you, Mr. Johnson," I said, giving him my best sinister look. "Please leave now, I have work to do." He was arrogant and was putting on airs. He was a sharp reporter, but he worked for a shrinky dink newspaper, hand-cranked on a century old mimeograph machine, that cared more about hometown America news like little league games and Memorial Day parades than hardcore articles about the Middle East or pending Federal legislation.

"This is a public library and I can be here all I want. My taxes pay your salary—don't you forget it." The annoying little man goose-stepped out of the library, slamming the door like a spoiled infant.

I rubbed my temples wondering why Shane couldn't keep his mouth shut because this would turn into a huge fiasco once it got into the newspaper. Gold fever in Waterville could prove to be a disaster of monumental proportions. We could get bounty seekers from throughout the United States swarming in here. We'd have to move fast from here on out. If only I could decipher the rest of the skin. Wash Loomis was too clever for me.

I spent the next few hours droning through my day until the phone rang; Shane was on the other end.

"Hello."

"Did you figure anything out yet?" he asked, in a rude way. I could hear Jessica yakking in the background.

"No, but I'm close."

"Can you come over to my trailer tonight? I think it would be better to work over here since we'll have heat on us if the word gets out."

"I don't have a car, and besides, if you had kept quiet about it we wouldn't have to worry. Lyndon Johnson was in here this afternoon and now it'll be in the *Crabtree Courier* for sure. I need to be alone so I can concentrate. I have your number. I'll call you as soon as I figure it out," I snapped. I was upset at the way he was talking to me. It was probably that Jessica's doing.

"Okay, but call me when you get anything."

I looked up from the desk and Gladys Rolander was crossing her eyebrows, angry at having to wait. "I have to go now, I have a customer." Gladys, at one hundred and two, was the oldest and nosiest citizen in town. I couldn't imagine being so old and so miserable. I'm afraid God wants to keep her alive just so I have to deal with her. I appeased her with a quick stamp of her book, ignoring her advice on a better type of ink that doesn't smell as much as the kind I currently use.

The phone rang again and I thought it was Shane.

"Hello. Waterville Public Library."

"Yes, I need to speak to Amanda Love."

"You want me to find Amanda Love?"

"I'm right here, baby."

I slammed the phone down on the little wiseass and his laughing companions. I can't honestly understand why boys find such triviality so hilarious. And they think women are hard to figure out.

Daisy Daring

The long day finally came to an end and I gladly locked the library door, dreading every minute of my life until I got the gold and built my own place where difficult patrons would be excluded. It would be so sweet, my own library, my own rules, my own books.

Just then I realized I hadn't seen Doodle all day, so I went to my apartment and came back out into the library with an opened can of tuna. I tapped the tin side with a fork calling, "Here puss-puss!" until the old fella came limping out from under the romance section. He was getting worse every day so I set the can down and let him eat in the library for the first time ever. I'd come back for him later.

The heat of summer bore down upon my bowler as I hiked down the road to the Food King with the black backpack I'd had since school. I carried the walking stick that I'd made out of a limb I found in the ditch in front of the library. Most of the people in town drove to Clinton to shop at the large fancy Tops, but since I didn't have a car, I had to settle for the not as nice but more expensive store in the middle of town.

A red Mustang convertible full of teenagers roared by, causing me to jump off the shoulder of the road and into the tall summer grass. My heart stopped as the white back up lights came on and the tires shrieked and smoked.

"Hey, witch!" a young blonde girl screamed from the back seat. "Is that your broom?" I gripped my walking stick. They laughed at me and peeled out causing me to choke on a cloud of burnt rubber and roadside dirt. I took off my bowler and waved the dust away from my mouth.

I stopped at the bank to withdraw forty dollars from my account using my ATM card. I use the word "book" as my pin. The heat of the downtown sidewalks crept up my leather pant legs, dampening my thighs as they rubbed together. I wanted to appear dark and threatening on purpose, the anti-cliché librarian. I started thinking that once I opened my own library, I'd wear even more outrageous clothes, tight jeans and one of those belly shirts all the young girls were prancing around in. I could pull it off since I had a pretty flat stomach. Seeing the open-mouthed stares and jealous eyes of the women and other townies would make the pain of another belly ring worth it.

I grabbed a dented grocery cart that had a clump of chewing gum stuck to the bottom of one of the wheels making it thump with every revolution across the light green tile floor. It was a sticky floor that felt like fly paper as I stomped across it in my cowboy boots. Would it kill someone to mop the Food King?

I bought Doodle's favorite tuna Meow Mix and a can of beef-flavored pounce for his treats. I grabbed a box of green tea, some lemons, and honey, as well as some bananas, assorted nuts, pasta, and sauce. I really wasn't a vegetarian, but I couldn't bring myself to buy meat anymore. One time I had turned over a chicken quarter and gagged at the sight of the bloody undercarriage. I was further grossed out when I bit into a piece and a ligament stretched from my plate to my mouth.

My pack felt a little heavy as I pulled the straps over my shoulders and jockeyed it until it hung just right. I tapped my walking stick on the rubber exit mat, pretending it was magic, and said— "open sesame." I bet people from the time of the Loomis Gang would've thought this contraption as the work of the devil.

I took one step off the sidewalk and ran into the mayor and his lackey Kicker.

Chapter 9

Beckon Call

Beckon Call was the name I had given this one snobby patron at the library who worked for the Clinton school district. She was a schoolteacher who lived in Waterville, but drove down the road to her job. She looked down her nose at me and treated me like I was her lackey. She'd ask me to do her photocopying, assist in her projects, and do research for her classes. She'd walk behind the counter and use my stapler, take my paper, use up all my pink post-it notes, and make personal calls on my phone. I was most annoyed when she actually put her feet up on my desk. She'd snap her fingers at me and ask me to "take a message." One of these days I'll fix this prima donna for good.

Mayor

"Well look what we have here, Kicker," announced the mayor, licking his cracked lips. His gargantuan gold ring was reflecting sunlight into my eyes. "Hey there Daisy, do you need a lift?" He placed his hand on my shoulder and I could feel a chill down my spine. His teeth reminded me of large white tombstones when he smiled. His toupee was impressive, but I still could see a dribble of glue under the edge. I hate myself for having been with him.

"No thank you, Bob." I put my walking stick under my arm and adjusted my glasses.

I tried to walk around them but Kicker stepped in front of me and folded his arms. He was almost seven feet tall and temporarily blocked out the sun, allowing me to see directly into his thick chest hair sticking through the enormous gold chain he wore around his neck. He inhaled his cigarette, then threw it to the ground, exhaling smoke directly into my face. "Hey sweetums," Kicker said, in that creepy lounge lizard voice of his. He thinks he's a big deal because he was the football hero of Waterville back in the eighties. I guess that qualified him to be the butler to the mayor. He's still stuck in that decade with his tight, open shirt, and parachute pants. Mayor Bob Plunk was the quarterback of the same team and now these two run the town like they were still in high school.

I was an unattainable back then, now I'm just another conquest for this egomaniac. The pair has not aged well with their bellies straining the buttons of their too small dress shirts. They still acted like the Greek Gods they used to be. On middle-aged men this was pathetic and sad.

"I hear you been hanging around with that no-good Shane Loomis. Is that true?" questioned his honor.

"That's none of your business."

"I'm afraid it is when a town employee is fraternizing with a no-good-lowlife Loomis. Why that person just might find themselves out of a job."

"Yup," agreed Kicker, nodding his shining baldhead in my direction. He took a drag on his cigarette, exhaled and then snickered.

He was nicknamed "Shit Kicker" in high school because of his cowboy boots. Somewhere along the line he dropped the shit from his nickname. I was the one with the boots now.

I gripped my walking stick a little tighter, preparing to knock this jerk's block off. I was ready to send the mayor's buckteeth down his throat when they both stepped aside.

"Whooeee. Would you look at the fight in this here girl," said the mayor, slapping my rear end as I walked by.

Kicker grabbed my bowler and when I went to get it he threw it over my reach to the mayor, making me the monkey in the middle, until I finally caught it and thrust it back onto my head.

Old man Collins was placing orange price tags on wine bottles with his hand-held marking gun and nodded at me as I entered the store. I grabbed the last bottle of Tug Boat Red off the shelf and threw a few of the slim brown cigarillos he had in the smoke display onto the counter.

"I'll have more of that next week," he said, spinning the bottle until he found the price, then clacked the buttons on his hand-cranked register. "The grape blight has kept down the number of Finger Lake wines available this year."

"It's my favorite. It's just the right mixture of tart and sweet," I said, placing a twenty-dollar bill on the counter. I placed the cigars in the small zippered pouch on my backpack to keep them from getting crushed and zipped the Tug Boat Red in with my staples.

"If the secret ever gets out on Tug Boat Red, I'll never be able to get it again. Lucas is a small vineyard and they limit the production of this wine. I'm afraid the large chain stores will swoop in and buy it all up."

"Thanks, Mr. Collins," I said and walked back out into the scorching sun. I was wishing I had a corkscrew to open my beverage here and now.

Daisy Daring

I decided to drink the entire bottle of wine in one sitting and get really drunk. I was at my wits end with the remaining writing on the animal skin. I took off my bent glasses and rubbed my eyes that ached from staring at the gibberish for hours.

I snipped the tip off one of my cigars and chewed the end, enjoying the flavor of the sable leaf. I went over to my kitchen counter and picked up the framed photograph of my father and me from when I was nine years old and was sitting on his lap smiling. I had my arms clasped around his burnt neck. I could still smell his Aqua Velva that he splashed on every morning. This was the way I would always remember him: the leader, the protector, the buffer between Blanche and me. I asked him one time what he saw in my mother that made him marry her and he said it was a tight black skirt and black stockings. Stockings with a thin black line up the back of her calves. He was smiling as he remembered.

I knew if he were here, he'd have solved the remaining puzzle already. I was feeling the buzz of a whole bottle of wine and had to sit back down before I fell and bent my glasses even worse. I was tired of looking at the Welsh lettering, beginning to understand why the language died. I leaned back in my chair and held the wine bottle to my pursed lips and gulped the last drops down.

Then I picked my cigar back up and lit it and caught something out of the corner of my eye.

"What the hell?" I said out loud. I leaned in close to the wine bottle. "Eureka!"

Chapter 10

Cornelia Loomis: The Loomis Gang 1865

Cornelia had seen Sheriff Filkins and his posse coming up the hill towards the Loomis homestead. She lifted her skirt and sprinted up the porch stairs and into the kitchen where Grove and Wash were playing poker with a few of the other gang members.

"Filkins!" she yelled, and turned to go back to the front door to run interference while the gang hid in the false walls and hidden rooms of the house. It was where all the stolen loot was kept until it could be taken away and fenced.

Filkins had declared martial law on the Loomis Gang, he was the only person hearty enough to take on the deadly Loomis brood. The gang had every judge, policeman, and politician on their vast pay-roll. Although it depleted a good portion of their booty, the bribery had kept them out of jail and had given the men license to steal with impunity. Their victims faced a vengeful gang that specialized in burning down houses if anyone dared place a claim against them. The Loomises had free rein to do as they pleased, that is until Jim Filkins became Sheriff of Waterville.

"I have a warrant, Cornelia, so stay out of my way," barked Filkins to the Outlaw Queen, waving a rolled piece of paper in his hand. His pock-marked face was red with fury and throbbing with impatience. Sheriff Filkins was ready for a confrontation. He and his band of twenty deputies dismounted their horses.

"Let me see it," she demanded, stepping down off the porch where the matriarch of the gang Rhoda was now standing. She was flanked by her other daughters Charlotte and Lucia. Rhoda slowly unfurled the paper and placed a spectacle in one eye and closed the other. Taking her time, she held the document up to the July sun to see if it was a forgery. It wasn't. She hadn't expected it to be, but she had stalled Filkins in order to give the gang time to hide.

"Just get out of the way, woman!" yelled one of Filkins impatient men.

"I don't think so," replied Cornelia, holding up her palm at the men and their drawn guns. "Nobody moves until I decide this is a legitimate warrant." Her education further incensed the posse, most of whom couldn't read. They were used to their women looking down at the floor and standing behind them with their mouths shut, not ordering them around, let alone being able to read. To them, a woman was more of a possession, not unlike a good raccoon dog.

"You've had more than enough time to see that this is a legitimate warrant," complained Filkins. He was so huge that he cast a shadow over Cornelia.

"I guess everything's in order," said Cornelia, handing back the warrant, nodding up to her sisters and mother, who stepped aside.

Out of the corner of his eye, Sheriff Filkins spotted Grove making a mad dash for Nine Mile Swamp. Filkins turned and gave chase, the Loomis' foxhounds were baying and nipping at his ankles as he raced down the knob. Filkins knew that if Grove made it into the dense brush, no man or dog would ever find him.

Filkins almost had his hands on Grove, reaching out, touching the crook's collar with his fingertips. He knew one more lunge and he'd have him, when suddenly he was tackled from behind by Cornelia. She was as fast as any man, even in her long dress.

Filkins watched Grove duck into the brush and closed his eyes in defeat. He knew there'd be no other gang member inside the house. The posse would have to regroup and come back another time.

"If you wasn't a lady, I'd string you up, Cornelia," muttered Filkins, angrily brushing the dirt off his pants.

"Why, Sheriff," she said, batting her deep blue eyes at him, melting his heart with her deadly stare. Men were always putty when she wanted them to be. She polished her spectacle with her pulled up dress while flashing her perfectly straight white teeth, a rarity in that territory.

"I say we take her in for obstruction of justice," said a member of the posse, walking towards Cornelia. He halted when Jim Filkins held out his arm.

"No boys, we'll come back another time." Filkins and the posse mounted their horses, tipped their hats and nodded to the clever Outlaw Queen. Filkins smiled at her, turned his horse, and led his men down the hill and back up the narrow dirt road, away from the knob.

Chapter 11

Daisy Daring

I stared at the wine bottle, unable to move. I had cracked the code and it had been so simple. I could see the reflection of the Welsh lettering mirrored in the wine bottle. Wash Loomis had written the last and most important directions to his buried treasure backwards. How brilliant, yet how simple at the same time.

It didn't take me long to decipher the exact location of the sinkhole that held the lost gold of the Loomis Gang. I memorized it like the rest, not caring if Jessica held a razor to my jugular for I would never reveal the location until Shane and I were ready to retrieve our fortune.

I shut off all the lights in my apartment and undressed for bed. I hugged my pillow like I was cuddling with a lover, falling asleep with Doodle purring at my feet, keeping them warm from the damp summer night.

A crash woke me up. I thought it was Doodle, until I sat up and saw my tabby at the foot of my bed. I waved my hand over the nightstand until I found my glasses and put them on. Someone was in my apartment!

My bedroom door started to creak. I pulled the covers over my head. My heart was in my throat as the floorboards moaned with each step of the intruder.

The trespasser was right next to me. They started to bend down so I closed my eyes, praying to my father to watch over me. I could feel a heavy breath coming closer and blowing over my face. I braced myself for the worst, but nothing happened.

Daisy Daring

It seemed like hours until I heard the door to the library close. I rushed out into the kitchen and everything was a mess. Papers scattered, drawers opened, food knocked over. I knew whoever it was they had been looking for clues to the missing Loomis gold. The madness had begun. If only Shane had kept his mouth shut. In any small town you only need mention something to one person and it'll get around the entire town before your tea cools.

Daisy Daring

I let Snider into the library and practically grabbed the *Crabtree Courier* out of his hands. The front-page headline was "Missing Loomis Stockpile Found." That damn Lyndon Johnson was going to screw everything up. I raced through the article, cursing under my breath until I finally handed the paper back to the waiting Snider.

"Miss Daring. Did you really find that lost gold?"

"No, Snider, I didn't. This man is making the whole story up." I couldn't believe that Shane had opened his big mouth.

"I'll be in the back, if you need me for anything."

I went back to checking in the returned books, stopping to get a couple of aspirin and a cool glass of water to help with my hangover. I was excited about the location of the cave; although, I realized that there might not be any gold. I wondered if this were the map my father alluded to. I anxiously waited for Shane to show up, knowing I'd have to meet with him in private, for the library was suddenly bustling with people. I was on display. News of the treasure had gotten around very quickly.

The phone rang and I slowly picked it up. "Hello. Waterville Public Library."

"Yes. I'm looking for a man with no arm and no legs. He likes to swim in the ocean. His name is Bob."

"Enjoy yourself, because very soon I won't have to put up with your crap little man. Understand?"

The phone was dead. Even if I had caller ID, I doubt I'd do anything about it. I had better things to do with my time. I'm sure these boys would be moving on to chasing college girls very soon and forget all about their crank calls.

It took all of a half hour after the library's opening before Blanche and my brother Don came waltzing through the front door. I hadn't seen my mother since our road trip to Remsen even though she lived just down the street. She had a new blonde wig with a crooked part—it resembled a miniature beehive. Her navy blue pinstriped suit was expensive, but somehow managed to look cheap on her.

"Good morning, sweetheart. Look at this place. A coat of paint and some replacement windows and I could get seventy-five for it." She set her purse down on the counter and put her cold hands on mine. I yanked mine away.

"Morning, Blanche," I said quietly, "What do you want?"

"I just want to get to know my daughter a little better. That's all. I was wondering if you could escape from this dreary place and come to breakfast with us?" She smiled, revealing the red lipstick on her teeth.

"I can't leave work."

"I don't know what you like about books anyhow," commented Don, picking up a copy of *American Tragedy* with his forefinger and thumb, as though knowledge were a communicable disease.

"I was thinking that we haven't spent much time together. I miss my daughter and I really enjoyed our little trip out to Remsen, especially since I assisted you in figuring out the Loomis map," she said, tears welling up in her eyes. "You don't think I feel bad for not being there after your father passed away?"

"You mean when you went to Florida with Glenn for a Caribbean cruise while I made the funeral plans? Or how I had to pay for his plot and headstone while you got the life insurance?" My father was so loyal that he never considered taking her name off the policy after the divorce, and even kept her name on his checking account.

"Please forgive me," she cried, holding her tissue up to her dripping tears. She leaned in and kissed me on my cheek, chilling me to the bone. I hated Don snickering behind her back, laughing at the look of revulsion on my face. "Remember that you're still my daughter. When people in town call you names, I defend you. You want to know why?"

"Not really."

"Because blood is the thickest between mother and daughter. I'll come back another time when you're in a better mood to forgive me." With that these two walked back out of my life. Don's finger was buried deep in his nose as he pushed the door open with his elbow.

The news of the Loomis gold had brought her back to see me. I wished I had a real mother. A Leave-It-To-Beaver, pearl-wearing, meatloaf-baking, afghan-making mother. Instead, I had Blanche.

The library was filling up fast with people milling around the aisles and mumbling—all staring at me. All wondering if they should ask about the gold. All wondering how they could get in on the action. Money made people wild with envy and desperation and I wanted no part of it. I wondered if it was someone here in the library who had broken into my apartment last night? Or was it Shane or Jessica, the mayor or Kicker, Blanche or Don? I just wanted my private library where all these creeps would be kept out.

Chapter 12

Daisy Daring

I hadn't heard from Shane in a few days and didn't dare call him on the phone for I was concerned about being recorded, always worrying about conspiracy in my life. I didn't like the Internet, cell phones or anything that could track my every movement, putting me in a time and place where later I'd have to worry about defending my position. Some would call it paranoia. I just called it good old fashioned common sense. I used my ATM card, but paid cash for all my expenditures so I wouldn't be a marketing statistic on some middle manager's desk in Pocatello, Idaho.

I opened the door to the library and Snider was waiting. Things seemed back to normal, but I knew I was still being watched by the curious and greedy who hung across the street, hiding behind their magazines, sitting on the bench in front of the barbershop, peeking their desperate eyes over the edges of their newspapers. Unemployment in Upstate New York, especially in the Mohawk Valley, was among the highest in the nation. These people needed a miracle to dig out from under their massive debts. I'd see them rubbing their rosary beads over the billion to one lottery ticket odds. They'd be telling God they deserved to win.

"Good morning, Miss Daring."

"Good morning, Snider."

I shut the door behind him as he stopped and turned to talk to me, breaking his usual routine.

"Is it really the gold Wash hid in Nine Mile Swamp?" He smiled and bobbed his head in glee.

"Snider, I can't discuss it right now. Keep quiet and we'll talk about it later. I may need your help."

"Okay." He went back to the place he hides while I tried not to think about where Shane and his floozy were.

My phone rang and I set my books down so I could answer it. "Hello."

"This is Jessica. When do you get off work?"

"We close at three today."

"I'm coming to pick you up, so don't go anywhere."

"Where's Shane?" I never got the complete question out for she slammed the phone in my ear. I wanted to tell him how wonderful and creative his writing was. It was exciting to read raw talent. I wished I could write that well.

I wondered what was about to happen. The rest of the day I day-dreamed about my life and all the wonderful changes that were going to occur. How Blanche, Glenn, and Don would be green with envy. I'll get a Mercedes and a mink coat.

I walked out with my backpack that held my cigars, the switch-blade, the skin folded in a large ziplock bag, along with some home-made trail mix, meow mix, and Shane's manuscript. Jessica was waiting for me, sitting behind the wheel of Shane's lime green Chevrolet Monte Carlo. It was loud; the engine clunked and the tail pipe spurted a dark gray mist. I climbed into the passenger seat, as I watched the gold fevered citizens of Waterville scramble into their vehicles behind us.

"Why haven't I heard from you?" I asked slamming the door, noticing Shane was not in the vehicle.

"You remember that you were supposed to call us? Just shut up. We'll talk when we get to the trailer," said Jessica, tapping the long ash off her smoke into the overflowing ashtray. The Jezebel peeled out, throwing me against my seat as the smell of burnt rubber seared my nostrils. I was a little worried about what was going to happen once we get to the trailer, way up on Loomis knob.

There were a few cars tailing us, but Jessica seemed to worry more about how her dry, bleached hair looked. She kept poking at the black roots.

The Loomis Gang had their house built on the highest hill outside of Waterville for a reason; to provide a clear view of anyone, such as wronged farmers and charging posses approaching. The original house was burned to the ground by Sheriff Filkins and his vigilantes, who were seeking the "California Solution," which was a hanging without a proper trial.

I leaned back and pulled out my father's pocket watch, adjusting the time and winding it. I rubbed my thumb across the smooth cool back before returning it to my pocket. I remembered when I was little and this thing looked shiny and new. I thought it was real gold. To me, this cheap timepiece was worth more than a million dollars.

I don't remember the trailer being up here when my father brought me up on the knob, years ago. The white trailer that Shane lived in had streaks of rust down the sides and was covered with scratches and dents. The front step was a couple of cement blocks. One of the side windows had a pane of glass missing with a piece of crumpled cardboard taped over the hole.

Over on the spot where the Loomis homestead had been was a miniature obelisk that was erected by the Loomises as a memorial. I remember my father telling me about it while he rubbed his hands up and down the acid-stained granite. They erected the obelisk before fleeing upstate New York, before heading back to New England. Shane was the sole local survivor of the infamous brood.

Before going into the trailer, I looked down the hill and saw a few cars at the bottom edge of the property. One man held binoculars while others stood on the hoods of their cars to get a better view. They held their hands above their eyes like sailors in a crow's nest, shielding their vision from the descending sun. They were too afraid, I guess, to step foot on Loomis soil.

The inside of the trailer smelled like a combination of burnt macaroni and cheese, ashes, and dirty feet. There was a sinkfull of dishes waiting to be washed and dirty laundry was strewn about the floor. I was surprised to see an elaborate silver candelabra on the folding kitchen table. I picked it up and I discovered it was solid silver. There were swirling snakes weaving around the base with red candles in their mouths. With both hands, I gently placed it back on the wobbly table.

There was an opened can of lima beans with a fork sticking out

63

of it sitting on the grimy counter. The place was so decrepit that I doubted even Blanche would want to sell it. I actually felt I was in the midst of real poverty, not my pretend poverty, but real down and depressed cash flow poverty.

We went into the living room and Shane was sitting on an old loveseat, wearing just a pair of jeans. His head was down; his hair hung over his face. He was holding a whetstone in his hand and slowly scraping a large hunting knife back and forth across the rectangular black rock. He stopped when he heard us. An old flowered sheet was thrown over the loveseat and I could feel a spring poke me in my rear as I sat down. I shifted myself but still couldn't get comfortable.

Shane looked up and combed his hair back, revealing a purple and yellow eye swollen shut and a bulging busted lip that looked like a lump of raw hamburger. He smiled and I could see he was missing a tooth.

"What happened?" I asked, in horror, not looking at Jessica for fear she'd smack my glasses again. I crossed my arms across my stomach and gripped my ribcage.

"You still got that switchblade?" he asked.

I put down my backpack and reached into my cowboy boot, where I had hidden it, and took out the knife, handing it over with no resistance. I was wondering if I had just made a huge mistake.

He pushed the button, releasing the weapon that glistened from the ray of light coming in the window behind him. He growled deep into his throat, then started working the blade across the sharpening rock. It was a better way to sharpen it than my brutal grinding wheel. Slow and steady.

"This is courtesy of your friendly local sheriff," he announced, pointing the tip of the blade at his face.

"Leech?" I asked. I was shocked that the sweet and jolly Pat Leech would ever harm anything. I once saw him scold a young lad for stepping on a grasshopper. With his wild white hair, thick unibrow, and granny spectacles, he reminded me of Santa Claus with a badge. Sheriff Leech would stop in the library every once in a while, and while speaking, would constantly be tugging on his belt that groaned under his large belly.

"Gold makes people wild," snarled Shane. He flipped the blade over and continued to stroke it up and down the whetstone.

"Well whatever's on that skin better be worth this," complained Jessica, pointing at Shane's battered face. "He got roughed up because of some punk he protected you from. Turns out to be Leech's nephew or something."

"Is that true?" I asked.

"I knew who the punk was. He used that little snot as the reason to push for the treasure. Did you find anything new?" He looked up at me, his icy blue neon eyes piercing me through the fallen strands of his dark greasy hair.

"Yes." I unzipped the backpack and set the folded skin with the Loomis map on his footlocker coffee table and sat back in his white plastic lawn chair. "I don't need this anymore because I have it all up here," I announced, tapping my forehead. "I know the location of the treasure and will tell you once we reach the hidden cave."

"I will tell you that Wash placed the gold in a wooden trunk and lowered it into a sinkhole. A cavern. He had known for years about this one special place because Plumb Loomis' prize beagle "Jeb" fell in while chasing a fox. They brought the man back up and he was dazed from the air."

"This is a load of crap, Shane!" yelled Jessica. I prepared to defend myself.

He held up his hand to shut her up. "We're going down into that cave in the next few days. You see how people are following us now, watching our every move? I was thinking we could wait until it died down, but it probably never will. The excitement will only build. I want my legacy now." He threw the switchblade past me, and I ducked. The blade stuck in the far wall of his trailer and was vibrating up and down. In spite of everything, I admired his passion.

"That's really mature," said Jessica.

"Hell, there's hundreds of caves and holes around here and near Nine Mile Swamp. You can stand out on the hill and see a million places. I hope that map points out which one," said Shane.

"I know the location up here," I replied, pointing to my temple again. "The creepiest part is when Wash came back with the swindled gold. He knew all along the cave would be the place to hide it so he and Plumb brought along another gang member and lowered the trunk down. Wash describes using at least one hundred feet of rope before it went slack. Then they lowered this unnamed gang member and removed the rope after he landed. They waited for weeks to see if the man would surface. I'm guessing that this was an experiment to see if there was another way in or out.

"Does it say if they ever went back to get it?" asked Shane. Jessica was snapping her fingers, clenching her teeth, and huffing air out her nose like a spoiled child.

"That's the thing that worries me because there is no guarantee the gold is still down there."

"What's our next move?" Shane asked, placing his hand on top of mine. His palm was on fire and I felt my neck hairs rise. I placed my free hand over my mouth to cover the gap between my teeth, another thing I'll fix when we get the money.

"We get the gear and we descend into the hole."

"How was my writing?"

He abruptly changed the subject, which was fine by me. I pulled the yellow pages out of my backpack, and carefully handed them back to him. "You are a talented writer. Your writing is riveting, desperate. You have the makings of something wonderful here."

"Wow!"

"You fool," laughed Jessica. "This liar is telling you this to get on your good side. You Loomis' are supposed to be so clever, yet you're tricked by this bitch."

"I beg your pardon, but my literary reviews are never for sale; at any price." I resented the accusation.

Shane pulled out three ice cold Utica Club beers for all of us to celebrate. I really didn't like beer but drank a few anyway. Within a few hours I wanted to go home but Shane was passed out in his bedroom and Jessica wasn't moving.

"It must be nice to be independent," she said to me, taking another sip. She threw the empty can into the paper bag with the others to take back to the store for the five-cent return. "I mean no stupid man in your life to mess things up."

"I like it this way. I can come and go as I please, without the interference of some dude making me watch bowling on television, or having to hear his philosophy on car engines." I snickered at the thought of a husband.

"That would be awesome, except you really need a man once in a while. Garbage has to be taken out and gas has to be pumped," she said, making us both crack up.

I needed some music. "You have any Johnny Cash?"

"You listen to that stupid stuff?" Jessica asked, stretching her chewing gum out about a foot, then shoving it back into her foul mouth.

"No, I was only kidding. You play what you want." I took off my father's bowler, and set it on the table.

"Why do you wear that thing when you have such beautiful hair?"

"I don't know."

Jessica put on some kind of rap metal that made my instep tap to the crunchy guitar and thoomping drum.

For some strange reason the drinking and music reminded me of the parties Napoleoni used to take me to up in Halifax. I was so shy I stood in the corner and watched the rowdy, immature, drunken-frat behavior, and loved it all.

It was getting late and I was worried about Doodle. He must be tired of being alone.

"Are you going to take me home?" I set my beer in the bag and pushed my glasses back up to the bridge of my nose.

"I'm too drunk to drive."

Jessica sat back on the couch next to me. "I'll take you home first thing in the morning. Oh, I just love your tattoo." My shirt sleeve was rolled up, revealing the small black widow spider I'd gotten years earlier.

"I'm going to get one on my lower back. Maybe a monarch butterfly or maybe a skull with flames wrapped with thorns." She put her hand gently on my cheek and said, "Now tell me where the gold is."

Chapter 13

Cornelia Loomis: The Loomis Gang 1865

Cornelia was awakened by the celebration. The gang was out on the front yard of the Loomis homestead cheering loudly. The late summer air was cool so she wrapped a woolen blanket around her shoulders and shuffled out to the porch to see what all the celebrating was about.

At least twenty members of the gang were drinking, slapping each other on the back, and firing their pistols into the air. There was no mistaking the flames from the village of Waterville in the distance. The fire was lighting up the whole valley. Cornelia turned to see her mother Rhoda, who had come out to watch as well.

"Dizzy," Cornelia yelled to the closest member of the gang. "What's this all about?"

"Good evening, Miss Cornelia," he replied, taking off his hat to address the woman that all the gang members loved. Her jet black hair fell down past her buttocks. Her sky-blue eyes glowed in the shadow of the celebratory torches. "There seems to be a fire at the Madison County Courthouse." By the looks of the fire, the citizens would have to let it burn itself out. No number of bucket brigades could halt that inferno.

Grove and Wash had recently been arrested by Filkins and charged with counterfeiting and thievery. The records and evidence were disappearing in the flames, thus keeping them out of jail. In the past, nobody would dare testify against any Loomis Gang member. Now with Filkins leading the charge, the citizens of upstate New York grew bolder.

"Mother, this isn't good," complained Cornelia. She stepped back up the porch, halting next to Rhoda.

"We always have trouble. We're used to it."

"This is different, Mother. I can feel a change in my soul. The power is waning. This isn't some pig farmer's house we're torching. This is a court of law. The Civil War is ending and I think we should relocate the gang to New England. We're living on borrowed time here."

"Perhaps," said Rhoda. She took a jug of whiskey from one of the gang members, swilled it down with one swing of her elbow, threw it off the porch and onto the ground, then wiped her smiling mouth with the back of her pajama sleeve.

"Filkins will never stop," warned Cornelia. Rhoda admitted that she may be right, "He still holds a grudge from when he was a little boy and his family's farm bordered this property."

Cornelia was surprised.

"Sure. He was a rotten kid. Your father caught him throwing rocks at the horses we had penned up."

"What did Father do?"

"He didn't lay a hand on the boy, but he had him arrested to teach him a lesson."

"I knew Filkins had it in for us. More so than anyone else. He's dangerous and he's not afraid of us," cautioned Cornelia. She reached out and took a swig from one of the other gang members' jugs.

"He's too foolish to be afraid. That man's a mindless brute with revenge in mind. He wants to destroy us. I'm afraid it might come down to him or us. He's got the law on his side and we might not be able to pay off every lawman in New York."

"Filkins is not going to like his courthouse burning down."

"Nope."

Chapter 14

Daisy Daring

I had left with Jessica laughing at me. She had told me that I could walk home since I couldn't trust her with the location of the gold. Then she threw me out of the trailer, forcing me to hike back to town. Well she better pray nothing happens to me because there goes her and Shane's new life.

I wish I had a flashlight because the road back to Waterville was pitch black, except for the light of the moon peeping through the thin covering of clouds. The crickets were screaming their best mating calls, drowning out all other nighttime sounds. At least maybe they would find decent mates.

I rubbed my bare arms that were covered with goose bumps from the damp fog that was seeping onto the road from the swamp. I prayed for a ride because it would take me all night to walk back to the library. What happened to all the idiots that had followed us? All I could think about was poor Doodle, hungry and alone.

I walked on the opposite side of the road from the Nine Mile Swamp. The swamp glowed in the moonlight. A veil of mist rose off it and seemingly crawled across the road, reaching for my feet. The swamp gas smelled like the skunk cabbage my brother had made me pick as a child just to be mean.

Just then the headlights of a car came over the crest of the hill. It was a dirty white Jeep with a zip-on top.

"You need a ride?" It was Lyndon Johnson.

"I'm heading back to the village." I had a chance to bail out and knew I made a mistake as soon as the Jeep started moving. He was drunk and was weaving all over the road.

"What's a nice lady doing out here all alone at this time a night?" He placed his hand on my upper thigh, squeezing and rubbing it.

"Just a little down on my luck," I said. I took his hand off my thigh, placing it back on the steering wheel. I reached into my cowboy boot and the switchblade wasn't there. I searched through my backpack while keeping an eye on his erratic driving, desperately looking for the switchblade. It seemed forever until I finally found the knife. If he tried anything, I'd pierce him like a roasted ham.

He slowed the Jeep down and came to a halt on a dirt road, just off the main highway.

"It's awful lonely in my house." He tried to lean in to kiss me. I placed my hand against him and felt his flabby chest.

"Get back on the highway and take me home... you're drunk."

"I know that you know. You know."

"What are you talking about?"

"The gold. You know." He slumped back and reached under the seat, I put my thumb on the blade release of the switchblade. He pulled out a glowing green bottle of booze.

"What's that you got there?" I was curious.

"Absinthe." He tipped his head back, his Adam's apple bobbing up and down as he chugged the illegal liquor.

"That's illegal in the United States, you know."

"Not if you have the connections I have. You want some? This is the real deal. It's got wormwood in it."

I took the bottle from him with the intention of throwing it out the window. However, I remembered the warm fuzzy hallucinations the green monster had provided. They called it "chasing the green fairy." It caused me to experience the greatest thrill I ever had with Napoleoni. And here in my hands years later, it called to me.

I took my t-shirt and wiped the bottle so I wouldn't get any germs in my mouth, and swigged down a mouthful. It tasted like licorice and spice, with a hint of sugar. I tried to read the label, but it was in some foreign language. I handed him back the bottle and coughed.

"That's what I'm talking about," he said. He laughed as he slid his foot off the gas pedal, causing us to bolt forward before he hit the brake again. He was clearly very intoxicated.

"Take me home now."

"C'mon baby. I won't hurt you." He tried putting his arm around me. I pushed it back.

I was starting to feel woozy from the Absinthe. I clicked open the knife and held it towards Johnson.

"Don't mess with me. I'm not in the mood."

He put the Jeep in park and took his hands off the wheel. He started weeping, slumping his head on the horn that blasted. I had to pull him back with my free hand.

"I'm so sorry, Miss Daring. My life is crap. I don't deserve to be in this town. I'm too good of a reporter to write about bake sales and flower beds. I'm talented and I'm wasted. My wife hates me too." He paused for a breath of air, sucking fast through his teeth. "She doesn't want me anymore. I'm just a husband of convenience." He paused to wave his arm in the air. "Just an errand boy to go here and to go there. No love, no comfort. No lust, just indifference." He slumped back down and continued to cry.

"Don't worry about it. Just drive me home and you can go sleep it off. We're all trapped in jobs we hate. Lives we didn't deserve. Like the rest of us, you'll have to accept it and suck it up." I pulled the knife back thinking I had him under my control, snapping the blade back into the handle but keeping it in my hand in case he started getting touchy feely again.

The Absinthe was taking hold; I had forgotten the blasting high this green concoction gave me. No wonder it's illegal here. I know now why Hemmingway and other artists swore by the stuff.

I looked at Johnson then closed my eyes and rubbed them. It was then that I felt his cold hand across the back of my neck.

The son of a bitch must have taken his foot off the gas pedal because I felt us moving forward as he tried to clamp tighter onto me. He leaned over and rubbed his moustache across my cheek.

I smashed the handle of the knife into his temple, and he loosened his grip on me. I jumped out of the Jeep before it came to a stop and my feet slipped out from under me. I was trying to get up when the man slammed his body on top of mine, sending me back down into the mud. I had the switchblade in my hand and pressed the button releasing the blade but I couldn't move because he had my wrists.

"Just tell me where the gold is."

He was out of breath and had to pause with each word. He was panting heavily and I could feel his heart pounding on my back.

"You let me go or I'll tell your wife. Get off, you fat little creep!"

I saw a white flash and realized he must've hit me. When I came to I tried to get up but knew I couldn't fight him off. I would've screamed but I knew we were way out in the middle of nowhere. I just wanted to live. He was searching my pockets as if I'd have the map to the gold in there.

"Now keep your mouth shut or I'll come back and finish the job. Besides, who's going to believe you over me? I control the press in this town, honey. I want that gold and you're going to cut me in on it."

He dumped my backpack out onto the ground, looking for the map. He got back in his Jeep and peeled out, dirt flew into my face. I stood up, wiping the tears away from my cheek with my mud encrusted hands. I put the switchblade back into my backpack and swore to never tell a human being about this. My soul felt dirtier than my appearance. I was mad at myself for getting into the Jeep in the first place knowing it was my own damn fault. An owl hooted above my head from an adjacent oak tree, its large yellow eyes blinking as the only witness.

I had decided right then and there not to report it or to tell anyone what had happened because I was afraid and, damn it all, I didn't want anything bringing more attention to our search for the gold. I laughed thinking of how my newfound gold would be used for revenge on all who have crossed me. I'd buy the *Crabtree Courier* and have Johnson write about lost cats and dogs and daycare finger painting critiques, real hell-on-earth writing that would squash his journalistic spirit. His wife hasn't anything on me when I'm angry. He's just fortunate that I abhor violence.

The ride with Johnson still left me five miles to hike in the cold. I walked humming my favorite show tunes that I used to sing with my father. He used to love to take me to the Stanley Movie Theater in Utica.

Chapter 15

Dewey

"Dewey" was the nickname I had given to one patron of the library who always came in to complain about the Dewey Decimal System. He claimed that he had invented a much better organizational system and insisted I use it and would go around trying to rearrange the books according to his system. Dewey had droopy eyelids, permanently bloodshot eyes, and spoke so softly that I could barely understand him so I'd just shrug my shoulders. He'd complain in the winter about being too hot and would curse at the thermostat and try to take it apart claiming he knew how to fix it. He'd complain in the summer of being too cold and would try to unplug the floor fan.

He had tried to move the bookshelves to a "better" location and ended up with splinters in his thumb from the wood floor. He'd sent the medical bill for the sliver removal to the town. The Board of Directors of the library yelled at me. When he'd get tired he would pass out in a reading chair and snore loudly. I'd have to poke him with a broom handle to get him to stop. The he'd wake up with more ideas on how I could improve the ambiance of the Waterville Public Library.

Daisy Daring

I sat in the bathtub scrubbing my entire body with a loofah, thinking that it could wash the Johnson scum off. I could always tell

Lyndon Johnson's wife that he assaulted me and tried to rob me, but I was ashamed and would rather bide my time and get revenge. Doodle was busy licking his paws, and ignored me when I walked in, only purring when I pressed the lever down on the can opener, letting him know food was imminent.

Daisy Daring

I was grim as I pounded the rubber stamp onto the black inkpad and brought it down upon the back envelopes of the returns. Shane wasn't the first man to let me down and sure not to be the last. Even the ever-reliable Doodle was distancing himself from me. He seemed a shallow version of himself.

The phone rang and I angrily said, "What."

"I'm looking for a carpenter's dream. A woman flat as a board."

"Is that the best you can do? Huh? Is it?" I slammed the phone down so hard I think the receiver cracked.

I wasn't in the mood for the mayor and Kicker to show up again. They walked up to the counter and the mayor set a white Styrofoam dinner container down.

"Good morning to you, little lady," the mayor greeted me, licking his buckteeth. I wanted to slap the toupee off of his smug skull. "You have any idea why we're here?" He was tapping his large ring on the counter.

"No."

Kicker opened up the container of steaming food. He took out a pair of chopsticks and started wolfing down hunks of meat dripping in sticky orange sauce. When he smiled, the sauce ran into his Vandyke beard.

"Well, now that we've seen you hanging out at the Loomis shit-box, and read the article in the *Crabtree*, we know why you're hanging around with that scumbag. You're going to cut us in on the gold."

"I don't know what you're talking about."

All the mayor did was nod his head and Kicker set the chopsticks down, wiped his face with a napkin, and threw the dirty paper towel at me.

I recognized the distress cries of Doodle as Kicker came around the bookshelves carrying the old fellow by his hind legs. The tabby was desperately trying to escape or scratch his tormenter, but was unsuccessful.

"Let him go, you big Cretin," I screamed as I rushed around the counter. The mayor grabbed me from behind and I tried to scrape my boot heel down his shin.

"Shhhh. Quiet in the library," he whispered, squeezing me so tight I thought I'd pass out.

"Miss Daring, are you okay?" called Snider. He had heard the ruckus from the back and had gallantly tried to come to my rescue. He was looking at the floor and wringing his hands.

"Hey, old man, go cut some grass. Vamoose," yelled Kicker, leveling his thumb. "Boogie." He took a step towards Snider, and Snider retreated. The two men looked at each other and laughed.

"Kicker here will take your cat over to Lotus House and have them slice and dice kitty, just for you."

"I have no idea where the gold is. Shane had an old document from the Loomis Gang, but it was nothing but ramblings. It didn't give a location other than Nine Mile Swamp."

He let go of me, and nodded to Kicker who threw Doodle onto the floor. "Hell, that's nothing new. Only a madman would go walking around in that swamp. But, we'll be watching you and if you do find the gold, you're going to cut the government in on its fair share."

The two high school has-beens stormed out of the library, past a little boy holding a copy of *Curious George*. I took the book from him, said "thank you," and ran around the desk. Snider was down on his knees, petting Doodle, who was lying down, panting. When the cat saw me, he bolted under the shelf and hissed. Another man in my life hated me.

"I think he's going to be fine," consoled Snider.

I nodded my head and placed my hand on Doodle's furry paw.

"I'm not stupid, you know," he said.

"I know that, Snider."

"I'm just a little slow. Takes me a little longer to get there, but it's worth the wait."

We both laughed and I wiped the tear on my cheek with the back of my hand. When I'm rich, these losers will get theirs!

I composed myself and went back to work, wishing I could kiss Shane. I was ashamed to admit that I liked him. It was probably because I had been starved of love for so many years. I was weak, but I knew I was too old for him.

The phone rang and I hustled to pick it up, turning my back to the patrons.

"Hello."

"Sorry I fell asleep last night. I guess you made it home okay," asked Shane.

"Yes. Yes, I did. Are you okay?"

"I think I'll live. That damn Leech beat the crap out of me and I still wouldn't tell him anything. I can't believe I still have people watching me from the edge of the hill."

"I know what you mean. I'm being watched all the time too," I replied.

"Well, I think we should wait a week or so and then go for the gold. We'll need to go to Utica and buy some rappelling gear so that we can get down into that hole. I think we'll also need someone else to assist us. You, Jessica, and I will be going down. We need some-one to watch. Maybe that guy that hangs around the library?"

"I agree. By the way, I thought you said last night that we need-ed to go down right away?"

"I'm hoping if we lay low for about a week, people will figure we have nothing and then we can make our move. Do you have any money to buy the equipment? Might be a few hundred bucks. We could pay you back from the gold."

"I can get it. And I'll talk to Snider about helping. We can trust him, he's a good egg."

"You really liked my writing?"

"Genius. No doubt about it." I hung up the phone and went back to my duties knowing Snider's involvement would be great for me. It would make the team even. I still didn't trust Shane, but I was eager to get to my fortune. I walked to the back of the library to fill Snider in on the deal, promising to pay him from my share if he would help us.

My daydreaming was interrupted by an elderly female patron

clearing her throat to get my attention. Her nylons were rolled down to her ankles and she had on glasses so thick she looked like a white-haired owl. She looked much like the old woman I had found slumped over dead last year. That was weird how that old lady was frozen over her favorite book. Dead! I had to have the undertaker pull *The Wizard of Oz* out of her hands so I didn't have to buy a new version. I thought it noble to pass away doing something you love.

"Miss, the bathroom toilet is overflowing."

"This happens all the time, no problemo," I said.

I performed the drill. I went to the broom closet, took out the clothespin and snapped it over my nostrils. I took out the yellow Playtex gloves that went up to my elbow and the mop. I took off my cowboy boots and stuffed my feet into the oversized rubber pack boots.

I was a renaissance librarian, transformed into the Roto-Rooter man. I kicked the door open with the heel of my boot and splashed through the puddle. I set my mop down and took out the plunger from behind the toilet and pumped it up and down. Then I pushed down the handle of the toilet and was thrilled that the water swirled around and disappeared. I swabbed the splashed-over toilet water, then I put my plumber gear back into the closet.

"Snider?" I looked around and couldn't find him.

"Yes?"

I jumped, for he seemed to materialize out of thin air, giving me a chill up and down my spine.

"I know I can trust you." I stopped talking and made sure no one was listening as I craned my neck around the aisle next to us. "We think we've found the place where Wash hid the stolen gold."

"Oh my goodness." He sat down.

"You have to be quiet about it. The reason I'm telling you is because I want your help in the recovery." I sat next to him and leaned in. I shut up when a patron came strolling by looking through some books, humming under his breath. As soon as he turned the corner I continued.

"You told me you didn't know anything."

"I lied to you. I had to. Look how these people are acting. Gold fever. West Nile greed disease."

"You can count on me, Miss Daisy."

"You're a good friend Snider." I picked up his cold, fragile hand that felt as delicate as an eggshell. I didn't know who was in worse shape, him or Doodle.

Daisy Daring

A week passed and Shane had been right, the curious had dwindled, especially with Shane or Jessica not coming around. I did a lot of research on mountain climbing, and cave exploring, so I could have some kind of idea of the equipment we needed, and how we would go about retrieving the loot.

I was excited because Snider told me he had been a mountaineer in World War II; although he claimed he fell and cracked his head open on a boulder and that's what led him to a life of cutting grass.

I found the work in the library was wearing me down as the days ticked by. When I have the Doodle Library in operation, I will pay someone to do all the dull stuff, while I compile my lists of banned books and unwelcome patrons, as well as one for those I'll allow to borrow my books.

I picture myself ignoring Blanche and Don pressing their noses against a cold winter window while I sip wine by the fireplace, smoking a Cuban and reading a little *Thales*, my Johnny Cash music would be drowning out their pleas for money. I'd light my cigar with a hundred dollar bill, just to annoy them.

My daydreaming was interrupted by a voice that I could never forget.

"Hello, honey dew."

I looked up, and Napoleoni was standing at my desk.

Chapter 16

Harry Daring

I remembered the time I brought my report card home at the end of sixth grade. My father glowed at my top grades and my perfect attendance certificate. Don's report card for eighth grade was a wrinkled mess from my brother's attempt to alter his straight Ds.

"Why bother getting good grades," my drunk mother had said to me. "You'll just get knocked up by some white trash and be living in a trailer, at sixteen." She dropped my report card to the floor and pulled the swizzle stick out of her highball and ran it down her tongue.

I could tell my father was angry, but he never raised his voice to Blanche. They were so different. I just couldn't understand what my father saw in her. She didn't bake cookies or practice soccer with me. She was too worried about ironing her suits and leaving day and night for meetings or something.

I found a note on her desk once and it had listed the most important things in the world to Blanche:

#1 Me, #2 Career, #3 Family.

It seemed that Don could do whatever he pleased and our mother would let him run free. My dad had to buy me outfits and hide them from her so I could look pretty at school. She said being poor built character and kept me from being spoiled.

Napoleoni

"What are you doing here?" I shrieked excitedly. Then I ran around

81

the desk and hugged Napoleoni.

"Hi Daisy, It's great to see you. You haven't changed a bit," he said. He pushed me back, looking me up and down. "I love your leather librarian look. A biker-chick book-checker."

He was a little fatter, a little balder, a little more wrinkled, but he still had the same frightening eyes that were light green with flecks of burning copper. His blonde hair had wisps of gray and was grown out and pulled back into a ponytail.

"I read about the possibility of the Loomis gold being found and was shocked to see your name mentioned." He held up a folded copy of the *Halifax Herald* that had an article regarding the possible discovery of the missing gold that had been stolen by an American thief over a century earlier. "I was in need of a vacation, so I thought I'd come and visit. It's been, what? Five years?"

"It's felt like twenty." I smiled, worried about his motives. I had to remember he cheated on me. Another man who'd let me down. I'm not a man hater, just a lamenting fan.

I still couldn't figure out how the *Halifax Herald* knew about the *Crabtree Courier* story, but I was happy to see Napoleoni, whatever the reason.

"I want to stay a few days and catch up. Is there a hotel in town?" He set his small suitcase on the floor.

I placed my hand on his and immediately regretted what I said. "You can stay with me while you're here." I couldn't help it because the old magic was coming back. I looked at his wedding band when I let go and he knew what was on my mind.

"Her name's Helen. We've been married for almost five years and we have a three-year-old son named Pierre," he said. He took out the family portrait. The woman looked a lot like me.

"She's very beautiful. Your son looks exactly like you."

"I know. I work for the Halifax Harbor Patrol, in the marketing department. I design the brochures and newsletters for tourists and such."

"As you can see, I'm doing what I was meant to do." I waved my arm around the dusty books with the crumpled binders and dog-eared pages. "Dalhousie wasn't wrong about librarians, that's for sure."

"Can you get out of here so we can talk?"

"I only have to work a few more hours then I'm off until Monday.

I don't work Sundays in the summer. I'll show you to my apartment and you can hang out there until I'm finished," I said as I walked Napoleoni towards my apartment. "If you get hungry, help yourself. There's a little greasy spoon across the street that has cheap eats."

"Thank you," he said, bending over and kissing my hand, like French-Canadians love to do.

"I'll see you in a little while," I promised. Then I shut the door to my apartment, and skipped back to my desk. I felt eighteen years old again.

The phone rang and I answered in my usual flat voice.

"Hey, how's it going?" asked Shane.

"Good. How are you feeling?"

"Better. I can open my eye now. I've been writing all week. I'm really excited that you liked my manuscript. Jessica's pissed because she hates reading and she has no interest in what I'm writing."

"She hates to read?"

"I guess she got by on her looks all these years. That's the Water-ville school for you."

"Hey, my father taught there. It's a great school."

"I know and he was one of my favorites. Your old man was a cool guy. I would've finished if I had more like him. He used to ask me all sorts of questions about my family. He liked me. He wasn't afraid of me. That's why I came to you in the first place. I figured you to be more like him than that wacko mother of yours. I'm thinking we might as well go get the gear."

"I have a visitor, so can we wait until Monday?" I was worried about his reaction.

"Who?"

"An old friend from college is in town. Don't worry, I'm not going to say a word, besides I need to get cash out of the bank to buy the gear, and it's closed until Monday." I could've used my ATM card but he'd never know.

"Okay. I'll let Jessica know that we're going to go on Monday. Later."

He hung up and I began to worry about loosening my lips to Napoleoni. I knew in my heart that the only reason he was here was because of the gold. He's no better than anyone else in town yet he's the last man I loved.

I watched the clock ticking with increased boredom and frustration wondering who'd invented such an evil device that ruled the world. I could just see Neanderthals standing by a clock with their clubs in their hands. At the tick of the clock they would proceed to brain their fellow cave dwellers. I was tempted to take the glass off the front of the evil thing and wind it forward, but the patrons all wore watches and would never leave until I threw them out at closing time. Once in a while I'd get someone who was engrossed in a novel and refused to leave, so I'd let them stay in the locked library. I didn't need that now. I needed a fast exit.

I finally was able to close the library and rush back to my apartment. Napoleoni was looking at the Welsh writing I had transferred from the skin. Thank goodness I had kept all the details in my mind.

"What's this?"

"Oh that? It's nothing," I answered, looking down at the paper with a disinterested glance. "Just some research to pass the time."

"It's really good to see you again."

"I know."

"You mentioned a place to eat. I'm really starving." I looked down and he had removed his shoes and socks and was wiggling his toes.

"Sure. Just let me feed my cat first. You better put your socks and shoes back on." I stood at my kitchen counter hand cranking open a sardine delight moist mix for Doodle when Napoleoni came up and grabbed my hips from behind. I jumped and dropped the can, splattering the pink mush all over his bare feet.

"I'm sorry." I laughed. I didn't think a man's touch would creep me out, but it was too soon from what I now call "the incident" with Lyndon Johnson.

"It was a long drive down here. I took the ferry across to Maine then took the highway here. I had to stay in Vermont last night because I was just too tired to drive any further. Then I had some really bad food from a roadside diner."

"Well, you'll like the Split Fork. It's cheap and good and it's right across the street. Just let me freshen up."

I went into the bathroom and rubbed a fresh coat of roll-on under my pits and brushed my teeth. I looked in the mirror and realized I hadn't worn any makeup in years. I fluffed my hair before I slowly lowered the bowler on top, tipping it to the side and winking at myself in the mirror like a dork in love.

"I love the hat," said Napoleoni.

"Thank you very much."

"Didn't your father wear one just like it?"

"This is his." I took it off and handed it to him.

He scrunched his eyebrows and looked on the inside of the hat, rubbing his thumb gently across the rim.

"This is one of the few things I have left to remember my father by." I took it out of his hands and placed it back on my head. "I wear it in memory of him. A tribute to the man that made me the librarian I am today."

"Uhmmm... Okay."

I walked across the street with Napoleoni and we headed to the Split Fork Café.

The people sitting at the counter stopped eating when we walked into the restaurant and began whispering and pointing. We took the booth in the far back and peeled the greasy menus from the blue Formica tabletop.

"What can I get you?" asked the waitress. She looked like she was still in high school and was wearing a faded pink uniform and stockings with a long run up the side, blocked with a dab of clear fingernail polish.

Napoleoni ordered the roasted chicken platter and an iced tea, unsweetened.

"And I'll have the vegetable platter and a glass of water with a twist of lemon."

"It's so great to see you again," gushed Napoleoni, reaching across the table and grabbing my hand. "This place is hard to find. It's really off the beaten path but it's a real pretty area."

"Wow, your accent has really gone away since I saw you last."

"Oh, that. I have a confession to make. I'm Canadian but I'm not French-Canadian. I used that fake accent to impress American chicks when I was in college. Also, my name is Napoleon, not Napoleoni. I added the vowel to make it sound more international. Actually, I was born in Hoboken, New Jersey and my parents moved to Quebec when I was a baby."

"That was a really rotten thing to do." I pulled my hands away from his and placed them under my thighs. The plastic booth stuck to my pants and made a splonging noise.

"I know. I was immature, especially when I cheated on you. I came all the way here because I've been guilty about it for years and wanted to apologize... I'm sorry."

"I accept your apology," I said. I took his hand back. I was simple in my forgiveness because I had to be. No water throwing in the face or slap to the cheek, just plain and simple forgiveness, another weakness of mine I'm pissed at myself about.

The waitress dropped our drinks off. Napoleoni's glass had a faded pink lipstick kiss on the rim. "Thank you," I said, not wanting to complain. I didn't want to make a scene.

"So you never married?"

"No. I just haven't found anyone worthwhile yet. I mean I haven't really been looking. My options are rather limited here. I'm not going to settle for someone just to settle."

"So the Fuarag really is an oracle."

Napoleoni was referring to the time we were at the Halifax Halloween Festival, and they had the old Celtic pie of whipped cream and oats, the Fuarag, that would determine your future. You delved in and plucked an item from the concoction and your fate was sealed. The person who plucked a ring would be married, plucking money would make you rich, if a man plucked the button it would mean he would be a bachelor for life and of course I plucked the thimble that determined I'd be a spinster. Napoleoni hadn't the nerve to try his luck at pluck. I remembered at the time I had said, "What the pluck?" and we both laughed.

The waitress brought over the chicken platter. Seeing the slaughtered bird made me gag but I had to admit it smelled really good. The vegetarian platter was nothing but an assortment of lettuce and limp raw veggies, with a tub of gooey white and green speckled dip. The Split Fork wasn't the place for a vegetarian, it was meant for meat and potatoes not tofu and bean sprouts. Napoleoni picked up the chicken with his hands and was tearing into it like a barbarian.

Chapter 17

Napoleoni

Just when I was starting to enjoy the conversation, Glenn Burke had to come in and bother us.

"Daisy, we need to have a talk," he said. He stood with his arms folded, leaning against our table.

"Not now, Glenn. I'm busy."

"I hope you're happy because your mother's in tears. I expect you to be nice to her and help her out." He was tapping his foot on the floor. I took a sip of my water, not looking at him, hoping he'd go away. "You're a selfish person."

"I'll talk to Blanche later, Glenn." He left and I took a deep breath.

"I see your mom hasn't changed a bit either. Has that guy married her yet?"

"No, and he never will. He doesn't respect her. I know he's running around behind her back and she doesn't see it. He's been mooching money off of her for, I don't know, twenty years now. Blanche suddenly loves me because of the possibility of gold." I could see Napoleoni's eyes light up at the mention of gold.

"Yeah, I was going to ask you more about that. I want to help you recover it."

"Napoleoni. Napoleon. Whatever your name is. We don't know where it is. An overzealous, umm, reporter wrote that in the *Crabtree Courier* and it must've been sent to a subscriber up in Halifax who in turn handed it to the journal. We have nothing. Is that why you came all this way? For gold and not me?" Looking at the chicken fat on his chin made me nauseous.

"I'm sorry. The real reason I came to see you was to tell you they've discovered the identity of the unknown child." He wiped his hands and face with a moist towelette. I pushed my veggie plate away with the heel of my hand.

"Really?"

"His name was Nicholas Barton."

Napoleoni and I had met, and first kissed, at the site of the Unknown Child, a mystery baby that Canadian sailors plucked from the frigid Atlantic Ocean after the Titanic sunk. The people of Halifax buried one hundred and fifty unknown survivors but had a soft spot for the infant floating face down-all alone, away from his mother.

"How did they do it?"

"They exhumed the body and all that was left in the coffin was a wrist bone and three teeth."

"That's morbid." I waved a fly away that was buzzing my ears.

"No, not really. They extracted the DNA and matched it with a cousin through the matrilineal line. He was thirteen months old, little Nicholas, when his mother, Lillie, refused to take a seat on the lifeboat. She had three other children lost amongst the frantic passengers and refused to leave the boat without them."

"That's so sad."

"I thought it was kind of selfish. She could have saved that baby and herself."

"No mother would ever leave any child behind." I looked down at my napkin, folding it into a triangle, knowing that Blanche would've left me playing jacks on the deck while taking the last seat on the last lifeboat herself. I could see her worrying that her ten-dollar shoes were getting scuffed and complaining that her view of the Titanic was blocked by the rim of some old woman's hat.

Chapter 18

Pete and Repeat

"Pete" and "Repeat" were the nicknames I had given to two fif-teen-year-old, born-again Christian patrons of the library. They'd come into the building wearing identical black suits, starched white shirts, black neckties, each with fake red carnations pinned to their lapels. They were boys in black suits, with black bibles in their hands, preaching to anyone who was reading books manufactured by the devil.

"Why are you promoting Satan's message with our tax dollars?" Pete would ask while Repeat would hold a copy of *Fahrenheit 451* in my face. "We pay your salary."

I doubted these two even worked, let alone paid taxes on their religious crusade.

They especially loved quoting scripture to me. I guess librarians aren't supposed to have a spider tattoo and silver rings on their fin-gers. I had more in common with Jesus, Mary, and Joseph, than those snot-nosed bible thumpers ever would.

They'd annoy people trying to read by asking, "Have you been saved?" And "Have you taken Jesus Christ as your personal savior?" I'd have to toss them out and they'd get upset and claim I was in cahoots with the devil, calling my religion "false" and "non-Christian," because I was Roman-Catholic. I had made the mistake of telling them my religion.

I'd laugh because if King Henry VIII didn't want a divorce, there'd be no other protestant religions. These two would say I wor-shiped idols because we had a crucified Jesus on our cross, and claimed we prayed to Mary, and that all Catholics were pawns of the Pope.

Daisy Daring

Doodle wasn't too thrilled about having another man in the house, spitting and hissing at Napoleoni before scurrying under my bed. What a good cat. I threw an old pillow and blanket on the couch, knowing I wouldn't sleep with a married man again. I made that mistake with the mayor years ago and his wife would never let me forget it, coming into the library with their spoiled son. She'd yell at me, just trying to get a rise out of me, so she could get her husband to fire me.

I only had a little wine left, but, fortunately, Napoleoni had bought some white Zinfandel on his way into town. He was driving a little purple Cavalier that he had parked out behind the library.

He went into the other room and called his wife on his cell phone telling her he missed her. I could hear him saying he didn't have the gold yet. He's crazy if he thought I was the same naive girl he duped with his affair and his fake French accent. In the morning I'll toss him out on his ear.

"Well my wife is glad to hear I made it to Waterville in one piece," he said. He sat at my table, tapping his pack of smokes on his palm.

"Uh-huh." I bit the tip off of one of my cigarillos and spit it into the ashtray. Napoleoni, the phony, clacked the top free on his chrome Zippo and turned the flint wheel with the same hand, lighting my cigar.

"Thank you for letting me stay here. Your tabby really seems to hate my guts."

"He's a good barometer on character." I exhaled a cloud of smoke into the user's face. He was still handsome but I was too strong to fall for his slimy moves. I'm not a college farm girl anymore. His James Bond attaché case full of maneuvers hadn't advanced one bit.

The phony French-Canadian took out a small square of craft paper and unwrapped a hunk of Limburger cheese and some raw onion. I had forgotten how he loved a toasted sandwich of these god-awful smelly foods. He took my frying pan out and sizzled the bread black, making my eyes water from the foul odor.

"That cigar reeks. Boy you've changed since we dated. Aren't you glad to see me?" He put his hand on mine and focused on my eyes.

"It is good to see you again. I always felt bad about the way we

90

broke off. I always wondered what would've happened to my life if you hadn't, you know." I wanted to say because he'd gone out with another woman behind my back. I was smiling, covering my teeth with the back of my hand. I took off my bowler and set it aside, fluffing my matted hair, then I adjusted my glasses.

"I apologized for that earlier. I know that if I didn't make the mistake of an affair, I'm sure you'd have been with me up in Halifax, and not back in this pit stop." He lapped the melted Limburger off the plate with his elongated tongue, making my stomach curdle worse than that evil cheese. "So, honey dew, you going to include me on your treasure hunt?"

"I told you before there is no gold. That reporter listened to a drunken Shane Loomis and exaggerated for the love of a juicy story. People love a good pirate story, especially when it's mixed together with a ruthless family crime syndicate. That reporter committed nothing but lazy journalism to write a story without the facts, making stuff up as he went along. I swear I don't know what's wrong with people."

I pinched the cigar between my lips, picked up my wine glass by the stem, and swirled the dab of remaining Zinfandel around, holding it up to the light while exhaling out my ring-pierced nose like a bull, zeroing in on my opponents red shirt.

I decided to play it cool instead of getting upset. "Yes, I know a lot about the Loomis Gang, but I do not know where and even if they had gold. You know how many people have died in the last hundred years looking for it? Well the souls of the greedy hang their ghosts over Nine Mile Swamp, and I'm not going in there with no idea where Wash supposedly hid it."

Napoleoni went to the couch, laid down facing the cushions, and pulled the blanket over his head like an infant. I was shocked that his maturity had been dwarfed by Shane. This hurt puppy boy routine worked on me before but not now. I went to bed, taking my art supplies and my zebra with me. I propped a chair against my door to keep the fake French-Canadian out, praying Doodle would use Napoleoni's leg as a scratching post while he slept.

I stayed up to paint my zebra. I had already painted the entire animal white and had to detail in the stripes, mane, and snout in black. My hands had started to shake a little recently. The quaking making it harder to get the fine parts as good as I wanted. It made me appreciate my father's handiwork even more, although an amateur could probably look at my work and not tell the difference between my carvings and my fathers. I could find too many mistakes in my own work. His was glorious and perfect and mine was full of flaws. My ark will soon be completed, just in time for a biblical catastrophe, a self-fulfilling apocalypse.

Napoleoni

The next day I couldn't get Napoleoni to leave. I had to get ready and open the library and he was right on my heels every second. I was expecting him to make a move on me last night but I guess I had neutered him. Maybe I wasn't as good looking as I thought I was. Maybe he really has matured and is faithful to his wife.

I reached the library, steady Snider was already there waiting for me to open the front door, with Napoleoni right behind.

"Good morning Miss Daisy," said Snider. He already smelled like gasoline, even before he mowed a single lawn. "Are we going to get the gold today?"

I looked down at the floor.

"Ah ha! So there is gold and you know where it is," shouted Napoleoni. He was pumping his fist in the air. "Well I'm not going anywhere until I get my share."

I felt bad for Snider, who realized he just screwed up and had water welling up in his eyes. I went about my duties, refusing to speak to Napoleoni, who just sat at the table near my desk humming some stupid song, strumming his fingers on the desk, conducting his own one-man air guitar band. My luck changed when Shane and Jessica came into the library.

"Who's this?" asked Shane.

Napoleoni just stood there with his arms crossed, all smug and arrogant, pinching his unlit cigarette in his pouty lips, staring from Shane's shoes up to his sloppy, uncombed hair.

"This is my old boyfriend from college—Napoleoni. Napoleoni, this here's, Shane Loomis, and Jessica."

"An honest to goodness Loomis? Nice to meet you," said Napoleoni, smiling like he was seeing a white tiger for the first time, holding out his hand that Shane refused to shake. "We might as well become acquainted since we'll be working together on the Loomis gold expedition. You know, the gold your ancestor stole."

Shane looked at Jessica, who gave me a death stare.

"What's he talking about, Daisy?" asked Shane.

"He barged in, Shane. I didn't invite him. He came down here from Halifax just to take the gold back with him."

Shane combed his hair back off of his face and he had a sneer that caused me to gasp. I saw that look before and I knew Napoleoni was in deep doody. "I'll give you to the count of three to hit the highway."

"You mean someone from this town can count?" joked Napoleoni. He was always using his humor to weasel his way out of it. He had always done that in college whenever he got into a sticky situation. He thought his wit and charm could get him out of anything. "I'm sorry, Loomis, but I'm not going anywhere."

Shane grabbed him by the arm and tried to walk him out of the library. The fake French-Canadian pulled free and walked back over to us, picking up the smoke that had fallen out of his mouth. He lit it in defiance and inhaled loudly.

"OK, we can do it the rough way if you insist," said Shane, and grabbed him by the throat. Napoleoni pulled free and knocked Shane to the floor. Then he set his smoke on a stack of books, and held his fists up like the old-time boxers did with their clenched palms towards their faces. Shane stood up, got punched as hard as Napoleoni could muster, went back a few steps, and smiled, revealing red teeth. He snickered before leaping onto the outmatched foreigner, hollering like a wild man, knocking a bookshelf over and toppling classic literature.

"Kick his ass!" yelled Jessica. She was throwing phantom punches a mere two feet from them.

Shane planted a few blasts to Napoleoni's face and he went running from the library. The purple car flashed past the front door saving me from further humiliation. In a way, I had received my revenge. Shane picked up the shelf and Snider helped him place the books back in order, including a copy of *Moby Dick* that had a burn scar from the lit cigarette.

Chapter 19

Harry Daring

I remember when I was eight years old and Don and I brought home our report cards. My father used to sit in his armchair, smoking his pipe, grinding the numbers in his mind. He had loved to figure out our grade point averages and what they would've been if we had a little higher marks. I usually had straight As and my father would glow from it, but Don always had Ds and Fs. My father, who was afraid of Blanche, would try to gently nudge him to get better grades.

"Don?" he'd whisper to my brother, who was eating peanut butter out of the jar with his hands.

Don would just walk away, lean against the window, and draw a stick figure on the pane with his dipped peanut butter finger. He wouldn't even look at our father. No fear. He wasn't brave. He was indifferent.

"Son, I think you could do a little better than this. You're smart, you just need to apply yourself a little bit, like Daisy here."

Then the ungrateful jerk said, "Mom said it doesn't matter because good looking people like me get everything on a silver platter. Besides, I don't want to be a geek with no friends like braniac here." He pointed his peanut butter finger at me. "She hangs out with Juggo."

I had felt bad for Juggo because all the kids pounded on him. I thought he was sweet. My brother was popular because he had acted like a jester. He was everyone's fool, including the teachers, who treated him like a monkey on an organ grinder. He was too stupid to see people were laughing at him. His dumbness made them feel better about themselves. Blanche let Don come and go as he pleased, showering him with praise and gifts, while I had to wear socks with holes in the toes and have her criticize every move I made. I could sense, even at eight, that she was jealous of me.

Shane Loomis

"We'll have to move on the equipment today," whispered Shane. He combed his hair back off of his face, tucked his shirt back in.

I decided to chase everyone out of the library early, including the mayor's wife, who I think had been spying on me for her husband. I think she was angry about my having been with her husband. I knew she'd run back and tell the mayor and get me fired. We had better find the gold soon because I will have nowhere to go.

Then Snider and I went and sat in the back seat of Shane's car. Hopefully, he'll be able to assist in picking out the right equipment.

I would use my meager savings to buy the gear, hoping I would have enough. I had told Shane I would give Snider some money out of my share for helping us. We knew we'd need Snider to help lift the heavy chest of gold out of the sinkhole, if its there.

We were headed for the City of Utica, where Adirondack Expedition Outfitters was located. On the way we stopped to eat lunch at the New York Pizzeria, a pizza shop that Shane adored. The guy making the pizza had an accent like he was right out of Brooklyn. Shane loved anchovies and had them loaded on our slices. He handed me a slice that seemed to stare back at me with all its little black eyes. I picked the dead fish off and placed them on a napkin. I didn't want what I'm eating to watch me eat it. Shane took them from me and tilted his head back and dropped them, one by one, down his throat. His Adams apple bulged with each pass of a little fish. He licked his lips and smiled when he was done. I had to say the pizza minus the fish was really good. Waterville had a few good restaurants, but no good pizza.

Jessica and I went to the bathroom. There was a urinal, a tiny hand sink, and a toilet that had duct tape wrapped around it. An "out of order" sign, written in magic marker on a piece of cardboard, was draped off the side of the tank. I thought my bladder was going to burst from the three diet cokes I drank, so I pulled my leather pants down and hung my rear end over the lip of the urinal.

"You really are something," exclaimed Jessica, her laughing echoing inside the cramped lavatory. She handed me some toilet paper that I wiped with and threw in the wicker trash basket.

I said, "When you have to go."

"Out of my way." Jessica, pulled down her pants and took her turn peeing into the urinal. "I want you to know Shane's not interested in you. All he cares about is his legacy. Oh, and the gold."

"I could care less about Shane. He's a child. All I want is my share of the fortune." I scrubbed my hands with a nubbin of brown soap, rinsing with ice-cold tap water. No hot water available.

"I see the way you look at him. You know that I know you got the hots for him," she said. She stood up buttoning her jeans. "He's my property. He's using you and you don't see it. You think he'll really give a share to you and that geek?"

I wiped my hands on a paper towel and threw it into the receptacle. "You'll never find it without me. Don't forget that."

Adirondack Expedition Outfitters was on Genesee Street in downtown Utica. The old building was painted a pumpkin orange with a tiny red sign on the front. A cracked Kayak hung crookedly on rusted hooks. A young couple was making out on the bench in front of the store, their spiked purple hair seemingly entangled like burdocks.

The inside of the store was overflowing with all kinds of equipment. There were hooks, several kinds of rope, oars of various colors and sizes, helmets, tents, clothes, and all kinds of camping gear creeping out of cardboard boxes. A clerk came up to us.

"Yeah, what can I get you?"

"We need gear to go down into a cave. We're going exploring. We need the works," said Shane.

"Have any of you done this before?"

We all looked at Snider, the one person who had done this before, although he broke his noggin doing it.

"Uhhh. I, um, did a little rappelling in the war. Had a little spill though."

"Well I'm happy to say the equipment has greatly improved over the years," the kid said, a small grin crossing his face. "You're going to need helmets, carabiners, harnesses, and rope." He walked over to the helmets and grabbed the most expensive one and handed it to Shane.

"We're on a budget," I told them, knowing I didn't have a lot of cash for all this stuff. After all we weren't making a career out of it.

"Oh, I see," said the clerk. "You can't put a price on safety but I'll see what I can do. He reached under the counter and pulled out a box of mixed helmets. "These are used and they go dirt cheap but I can't vouch for their reliability. Here's some lights to see where you're going. They strap onto the front of the helmets. I'd also bring a couple of hand flashlights if I were you."

We pawed through the helmets trying them on, looking for the perfect fit. I found a nice white one and Shane settled on a red one with flames painted on it. Jessica loved a purple speckled one that had a small crack in it.

"In my day we didn't wear helmets," proclaimed Snider.

"No kidding," said Jessica, getting a laugh from everyone including myself. I covered my mouth with my hand so sweet old Snider wouldn't be hurt.

The clerk threw a bunch of the blue carabiners into a box and then had us try on harnesses for size. He only had one kind so we couldn't save money there. I slipped my cowboy boots through the straps and pulled them up my leather-covered thighs until they were snug around my rear end. The clerk made sure they were the correct fit, explaining the fit was crucial if we didn't want to slip out and fall.

He then walked us over to the rope section. I noticed he had a tattoo of a black sun on the back of his neck that was partially covered by his hair and surrounded by what must have been thousands of freckles.

"How far down are you going?" He looked at Shane. I could tell that pissed off Jessica. After all I had the money, and he wouldn't even look at either of us. I was older and used to men thinking women had no brains when it came to almost anything.

"About two hundred feet," replied Jessica. She had just read my mind.

The clerk picked up a big roll of white rope with blue stripes on it and handed it to Shane. "This here's static rope and cannot be used for mountain climbing. It has no rebound. It's made for ascending but can be used for going down as long as you're careful. This is cheaper than the keenmanted rope, and I have more than enough for the depth you're talking about."

I asked, "What does that mean exactly?"

"Well, if you slip and fall, static rope will not stretch like a rubber band. If you fall far enough, you can snap your backbone like a twig. You'll also need a gringris device for each of you. You hook this on the rope and snap yourself down and back up one click at a time. These are simple to use. Just run the rope through and the weight of the person will hold them in place. Do you have any questions?"

We all looked at Snider for his expert opinion and he retreated like a turtle into a shell, frowning and pumping his shoulders up and down.

"We'll take it all," announced Shane.

"OK," said the clerk. "You know I can give you the name and number of some experienced climbers that could assist for a small fee. Interested?"

"Thanks, but we got Simon here," smirked Jessica, leveling her thumb at Snider.

"I'll sell you this gear but remember we aren't responsible for any injuries."

"Don't worry about it. Just ring us up," ordered Shane. "And throw in three of them two man tents." He stepped back so I could drop the stack of twenties on the counter. We carried our gear out and placed it in the trunk of Shane's car. I was eager to get my fortune so I wouldn't have to deal with this bunch or the stupid library patrons anymore. I took off my glasses and bent them a little bit, but they still sat crooked on my nose, giving me a headache from looking through a warped view.

Daisy Daring

I hated being under the curse of Juhannes Guttenberg, father of moveable type, hence all printed books. He was the baby step to the first amendment that I feel is a crock. They should add another amendment to restrict its usage to educated people because most of the people I met and went to college with could barely spell Dick and Jane, let alone know the ramifications of free speech. I'd like to muzzle all the uneducated. The Doodle Library will be my first taste at exclusion, and I'll love every minute of it.

We could see a cloud of black smoke a good ten miles from Waterville, and wondered whose house was on fire. We could hear the screaming sirens way before we turned the corner and realized the Waterville Public Library was ablaze. Shane pulled up and I bolted from the car, but was held back by a chubby volunteer firefighter who couldn't even button his flame retardant jacket around his oversized beer belly. Waterville, like most small towns in the Mohawk Valley, couldn't afford a paid fire department and had to rely on volunteers to hand fight fires.

I was panicky. I yelled, "My cat!" I was trying to get out of the powerful man's grip, his helmet came off and clacked onto the pavement. My bowler flew off in the scuffle.

"Lady, calm down. We saved your cat."

He let go and walked me around the truck and there was Doodle in one of those carrying cases meowing his little head off. I sat down and held the carrier, and watched as my whole life went up in flames. The fireman came back and handed me my hat. All the firemen could do was keep the fire from spreading. The library couldn't be saved.

I cried, for the only pictures I had of my father were in there. I had the only proof of his mortality, proof of his existence, which was now wiped clean from this earth. My Noah's Ark was cooked. I pulled my father's pocket watch out of my front pocket, turning the brass knob, fingering the cheap trinket that to me is priceless. Everything I owned was gone. I was both homeless and jobless.

I felt a hand on my shoulder and I looked up to see Snider just as upset as I. The library was his ritual, his sanctuary from all the name callers who had to be silent in front of him. I knew they'd never rebuild and I realized that damn gold had better be in that hole in the ground.

I could hear Jessica's big mouth over everything and I turned to see Shane bent over a squad car, being handcuffed by Sheriff Leech.

"What a shame. Damn shame," said the mayor. He was standing right behind me. He was talking to Kicker, who had a big smile on his face.

"Yes, boss, it's too bad," he said. He was stroking his beard with a big jack-o-lantern grin.

"Why, hello, Daisy. I'm glad to see you and your pal made it out okay," chortled the mayor. "Since you have nowhere else to live, I have a little place down in Deansboro I could let you have. No charge. What do you say?"

I was just about to accept the offer when Jessica came over and grabbed me by the armpits, helping me to my feet. "Get lost. She's staying with me." We walked over to Shane's car, stepping over the hoses, dodging the scattering firemen. The entire town was out now silently watching the destruction of their only learning center. They stared knowingly at the sight of the Loomis evil seed sitting in Sheriff Leech's squad car.

"Hey, there's no way you can blame Shane for this, he was with us, he's being discriminated against because he's a Loomis."

A group of teens were nearby laughing and hooting at the fire. I could hear them saying it was time to break out the grocery cart of marshmallows from the Food King for a little party.

Chapter 20

Cornelia Loomis: The Loomis Gang 1865

The Civil War had ended. Cornelia knew the returning veterans would be angered at the Loomis Gang and the riches they had acquired during the war. They had, after all, become wealthy off the blood of their neighbors. The recent burning down of the Madison County Courthouse made things even worse. The sheriff had no proof, but everyone in the area knew the Loomis Gang was to blame.

"Mother, I'm worried about the veterans, and their reaction to our fame and fortune," said Cornelia. She was leaning over the fence feeding apples to the horses.

"Nonsense, child. Your brothers have put the fear of God into these people and no worn out war dogs will make any difference."

"Mother, when we were in town Charlotte was in the dry goods store and overheard a few of the men talking with Filkins. Talking about taking the gang down. These northern soldiers killed their own brothers in bloody battles, they certainly aren't going to be afraid of a few backwoods bandits on horseback with tin revolvers. They could care less if we set the entire county ablaze. They've been to hell and back."

"Your brothers already know about the vigilantes. Their little club's got more to do with men drinking moonshine in the back of a shack, playing cards, and smoking cigars, than it does with chasing down a group of bandits," retorted her mother. She came and stood next to Cornelia and took her hands. "Besides Filkins has been silenced by the judges, politicians, and lawmen on our side."

"I know that we spend a lot of our money bribing these people, but my worry is these veterans will take matters into their own hands like they did on the battlefield. I know Wash brought that large trunk of gold with him back from the Northern territory. Maybe we should cash it in and move back to New England—where you and Father came from."

Rhoda continued, "Wash has that hidden in a place nobody will ever find. We'll sell when the time is right. We're not afraid of these men and their peg leg leader. Filkins is a sick man on a quest of self destruction."

"We are all a bunch of damn fools," Cornelia declared.

"Of course we are," Rhoda agreed.

"Who's that in the house?" asked Cornelia.

"Frank and Jesse James," said Rhoda. She waved a butterfly away that had fluttered in her face. "They're outlaws from out West. They're bringing some goods to exchange. We barter with them and they ask advice from Wash. They're good boys. We're looking to extend our business a little further than New York State. We're going to have a little celebration tonight to discuss the possible merger of two powerful gangs."

"I still think we should be more concerned with Filkins," worried Cornelia.

"Nonsense."

The James Gang

The men had placed some picnic tables on a plateau near the bottom of Loomis knob and had started a campfire. They placed oil lanterns on the tables and helped the ladies bring down the jugs of lemonade and beer. The food had been cooked in the main house so all that had to be done was to warm it by the fire.

The Loomis ladies sat at one table while Jesse and Frank James sat at another talking with Wash, Grove, and Plumb. A few of the Loomis and James Gang members were laughing while throwing large knives at each others' feet, trying to see who'd get stuck.

John Sullivan was playing his fiddle, everyone began to tap their hands on the table and a few stomped their feet. Cornelia noticed that Jesse was looking at her with a "big ole smile" on his face.

The most famous criminal in the land moseyed over to the table.

"May I have this dance, miss?" He held out his hand to Cornelia, who looked at it, then looked at her mother and sisters who were all nodding. Jesse was raw, rugged, and much younger than she, but he was gentle with Cornelia, holding her hand in the air as they strolled across the tall summer grass. They walked into the middle of the makeshift dance floor and the other gang members stepped aside. The two spent the rest of the festival laughing, dancing, and drinking together.

The next day Cornelia came out onto the front porch dressed in her pants and button-up shirt, her long hair swept up under a hat. She had some horses to alter before they were to be traded away. One of Jesse's gang members climbed the wooden steps.

"Well looky here. Ain't we cute all dressed up in daddy's clothes." He spit a greasy pool of tobacco juice off the side of the porch and wiped the drool off his chin with his stained sleeve.

Cornelia was used to gang members teasing her, but this western outlaw was crude and smelly. She tried to step around him, but he blocked her path.

"You might want to put a skirt on and make me some fixin's. Go on now. Back to the kitchen." He gestured towards the house. Cornelia tried one last time to get around him when he placed his dirty paw on her shoulder, knocking her hat off.

Cornelia punched the thief as hard as she could in the nose, causing him to fall backwards over the porch railing. The man pulled his pistol as soon as he stood up, but saw no fear in Cornelia's eyes as she took a step towards him and spit.

"Eat lead, bitch!"

Out of nowhere, Jesse appeared and placed the barrel of his pistol against the underling's temple. He had moved so fast that it caught Cornelia off guard.

"I think you owe the lady an apology."

"Oh, I'm sorry, miss." The gang member put his pistol back into his holster and walked away with his head down.

Jesse walked up the steps and picked up Cornelia's hat. He brushed it off, and handed it back to her, smiling.

"Boy, you're a fist full of hot buckshot!"

"Thank you, Jesse." She lifted her hair back up and placed the hat back on her head. "I can take care of myself."

"I can see that. Is Wash in? I have to ask him something before me and the boys hit the trail."

Jesse asked Wash if he could have Cornelia as his wife. Wash told him it was okay with him, but that nobody gave Cornelia permission to do anything, it was entirely up to her.

Cornelia was stringing the potatoes in the barn for the bleaching of the horses when Jesse appeared. He dismounted and came into the barn, taking off his hat.

"Miss Loomis."

She stood up and smiled at the ruggedly handsome thief.

"I was wondering if you'd be my wife?"

"Are you planning on staying?"

"No ma'am. We traded our goods for the Loomis'. Now we have to get back to our home territory. I want you to go with me out West."

"I'm sorry." Cornelia clasped her hands in front and looked at the ground. "I can't leave my family."

Jesse took her hands and got down on one knee. "I understand your loyalty and I love you for it. I don't want to take you from your family. Promise me you won't marry and I'll come back to get you."

"Yes, I'll wait for you."

"Good," he said. He stood back up and put his arm around the small of her back. He heard snickering and glanced at Frank and the rest of the gang who quickly turned their heads away.

"You'll come back and marry me?"

"Promise me you'll never marry another man until I return."

"I promise."

He leaned in and kissed her. Cornelia felt torn but she couldn't leave her family.

"I love you," he whispered into her ear.

"I know, I love you too."

"I'll be back in the spring."

Cornelia held back the tears as Jesse mounted and rode off. He never made it back to Loomis knob. She never saw Jesse James again. And she never married.

Chapter 21

Shane Loomis

Snider had us drop him off at his shack of a house. I never knew anyone who lived in a woodshed by the side of the Oriskany Creek. The shed was bleached gray from years of no paint and you could see clear through the cracks in the walls to the other side. When he opened the door to go in I could see hoses, lawnmowers, and gas cans in his way. We told him we'd come get him as soon as Shane got out of jail then we'd have to be ready to move fast.

Jessica and I went back to Shane's trailer to wait for his phone call from jail. There was no way they could pin the library fire on him because it happened while we were buying our gear, although I knew he wouldn't tell any details because revealing our purchases would tip Leech off that we have the location of the treasure.

I was bored and wished I had a chunk of basswood and my whittling knife. I always mellowed when I carved. I was trying not to think about my lost carvings. Most of them had been done with my father and would be worthless to anyone else, but to me they were more valuable than that stupid gold. Doodle rubbed against my legs. He had a scared look in his eyes just like he did the day I found him abandoned on the front steps of the library. I guess the jerk who left him figured me to be the cliché librarian and so I needed a cat.

Yup, that's me—a cliché. I rubbed my leather pants with one hand, tugging my hoop nose piercing with the other.

Shane called to tell us that his bail had been set at five hundred dollars, which would eat up the remainder of my life savings. But I had no choice but to bail him out of the Oneida County Jail.

Sheriff Leech was standing at the clerk's desk with his arms crossed as we lay the cash down on the desk to spring Shane. His white eyebrows were knit in a sneer, his teeth were grinding together, his nose was pulsating red. I never had seen this gentle man so angry.

"You'd better not find any gold," he warned, looking directly at us.

The deputy led Shane out and Filkins removed the handcuffs while Shane just looked straight ahead.

"If I find out you set the library on fire I'll break your damn fingers, every one of them. He says he was out with you ladies picking blackberries over in Sampson Meadow. Is that true?"

"Yes," snapped Jessica. "You had no right to arrest him. He was nowhere near that crappy library."

"Just don't you leave town before you see the judge." Leech put his hand on his revolver. "Now get the hell out of here. And, Miss Daring, I'd be careful if I were you. You have no idea of the kind of people you're playing with."

Shane was roughed up again as a result of the backwoods police brutality. He took a cigarette from Jessica and lit it before we all climbed back into his car and headed for the trailer.

"Are you okay, honey?" asked Jessica. She was rubbing his back while he drove. He didn't open his mouth until the jail was out of sight.

"Those bastards are going to pay for that. They made me strip and did a cavity search. Then they covered me with lice powder and put me in a cell with some crazy biker who kept picking fights with me," he complained, holding up his hands to show his bloody knuckles. "Leech and his men just stood outside the cell laughing."

"Daisy, I'll tell you what, the information hidden in that brain of yours better be worth all of this. I don't want to worry about going to bed on an empty stomach no more. I would love to have at least one pair of socks and underwear without holes in them. Maybe I'd even like to write for a living." Shane looked in the rearview mirror and smiled at me.

"That's a stupid dream," replied Jessica. "You're a dummy."

I didn't think it was stupid at all. I honestly felt he had talent. I secretly laughed at all the would be writers that would bring their manuscripts into the library for me to critique, as if I knew agents, editor, and publishers.

We went and picked up Snider and Shane told us we were heading into the swamp that night. We had people following us again and some of the onlookers were still hanging around the Loomis knob. I saw Kicker sitting in his pickup truck with Lyndon Johnson saddled next to him. There was a pile of junk food containers in the dirt next to the pickup. It was an evil partnership if I ever saw one.

Our plan was to wait until dark and then duck out of the trailer and head into Nine Mile Swamp, losing anyone who dared try to follow us. We knew once we got a few hundred feet in, nobody would be crazy enough to follow, especially in the dark.

"We better bring the cat," said Shane. "I'm afraid if we get away, they'll burn down the trailer and everything in it."

"I think it's a good idea," I said. "He already lost one of his lives in the library fire."

We packed food, the gear, and tents into garbage bags. We put Doodle into his portable house which made him hiss and whine. I wish I could explain to him that this was for the best. The stress was showing in his heavy breathing. I could also smell a little urine that wasn't him marking his territory, but frightened pee spraying.

We shut off all the lights and huddled together in the living room discussing when we would move. We decided that at the stroke of midnight we'd go into the deadly swamp with Shane leading the way.

"What direction do we head in first?" asked Shane.

"Wash wrote that you had to head 'de' from the back porch of the homestead. That means south." I whispered for fear we were being listened to.

"There's an old trail they used when they went to hide their stolen horses. I know right where he was talking about. They had a makeshift bridge made out of some old wooden planks."

"Then what?"

"We go one hundred rods in and turn 'dwyrain', which means west, at a marker, an upside down horseshoe nailed to a tree."

"A what? A rod? How the hell long is that?" snapped Jessica.

"A rod is five and a half yards or sixteen and a half feet," replied Shane.

"That's not right," said Jessica. She seemed pissed that Shane knew something she didn't.

"Yes, it's correct," agreed Snider. He was looking at the floor and kneading his hands.

"Who asked you, idiot?"

I intervened. "He's right, Jessica."

"Whatever you say, eggie."

"I think I may know where that marker is. I've roamed those swamps since I was a kid. There's some dangerous quicksand around, so everyone walk single file behind me," ordered Shane. "If I'm correct, there's a small flat patch of grass near there where we can pitch our tents. It'll be safer to move to the cave in daylight."

"What if some of those people down there follow us?" asked Snider, talking into his palms.

"They'd be fools if they did. We'll get a couple of turns in and no one will be able to track us, not even with hounds," said Shane. "The swamp gas throws off their noses."

"Are we sure there's even gold down in this damn hole?" asked Jessica.

Everyone looked at me, the decipherer, supplanter of my father as the preeminent expert on the Loomis Gang and the map, the only quasi-Welsh reading person here. "There's no guarantee of anything. We do know for a fact Wash found gold and brought it back here. But the thing about Wash is that he was a practical joker," I added, standing up to adjust my glasses.

"Legend has it when the Loomis Gang burned down the Madison County Courthouse, that Wash stepped out of the shadows to help the bucket brigade. He then manned a hose, yelling to everyone what a damn shame such a wonderful example of government efficiency was going to waste.

The answer to your question, Jessica, is that we won't know until we get down in there. My father told me there were fake maps. The extent to which Wash went to write on the skin and the language, and the way he hid it, I'm pretty sure this one is real. I think he got the idea to hide the map from Captain Kidd. I was reading about the pirate and he had maps drawn in obscure languages that were difficult to interpret and would hide them in his house. So I'm pretty sure this is the real thing."

"Are we all going down in there?" Jessica asked.

Everyone looked at Shane. "Snider will be staying up at the top, but the rest of us will go down in. We need Snider to haul up the gold," he said. He went into the other room and came out carrying a couple of walkie talkies. "Here, Snider, take this." Shane turned it on and showed Snider how to operate it. "You might not hear our shouting when we get down in the cave. I just put fresh batteries in these so they should be clear."

I admired Shane's leadership on this expedition. He had written a list of everything we'd need and he had looked over all the gear.

"Everyone come here," he ordered. We all gathered around Shane and he bent down on one knee. He was a quarterback leading the huddle. "Once we go down in we won't come out without our fortune. Dead or alive, we're going to get the gold. We know these people at the bottom of the hill are watching us so we'll have to move quickly. They'll have to kill me to get that gold away from me."

We all walked away in silence knowing we were about to embark on an expedition that would change our lives forever. In a way I wished Ofnadwy was here to place her hand on my shoulder and guide me. Somehow I knew we'd never be the same after we came back out of that evil swamp, the swamp that had already claimed the lives of many fortune seekers. I wasn't as worried because we had a ringer in the last of the Loomis Gang leading the charge.

I tried to get Doodle to come out of his box to eat but he refused. His single white fang bobbed up and down with his panting. He crouched down on his haunches, emitting a low growl like some invisible gremlin was poking at him. It was disturbing to watch and I had to keep him away from the others. Perhaps he knew we were going to haul him into the swamp. I agreed with Shane not to leave him here for the mayor's henchmen would surely come back and set this place ablaze after we lost them in Nine Mile Swamp.

I took out the switchblade from my backpack and put it in my boot. My backpack had other provisions like bottled water and a zip lock baggie of Doodle's favorite Meow Mix. I put on a light coat because, even though the summer temperatures were in the nineties, the nights of the Mohawk Valley were still cool and damp. Shane gave me a pillow and blanket bundled together with rope that I slung over my shoulder. I wound my father's pocket watch, placed it back in my front pocket, then rubbed the bowler for good luck and then placed it on my head.

We looked like a bunch of refugees. No fancy Mt. Everest backpacks for us; but we did have the only guide in the world who could lead us safely in and out of the dreaded swamp. We turned off the lights and watched the opportunistic group of onlookers at the bottom of the hill with their flashlights bounding around like fireflies. They knew we were going to move soon and they were as anxious as we were to get the game in play. By the time the clock chimed midnight we were ready to move.

Chapter 22

Daisy Daring

We lined up single file behind Shane in his trailer. He had tied a six-foot length of rope to himself and then to everyone else, instructing each of us to hold on. He claimed that this style of marching was used by his ancestors. I had never heard of it in all my fathers' tales or in all the archives I went over regarding the Loomis Gang, but, sometimes oral traditions are the strongest and most reliable. I knew better than anyone that the pen could lie. A writer has more power than any politician, emperor, or sheik. An archivist could alter history with a couple of keyboard strokes.

Shane had the trash bag full of gear in one hand and Doodle's carrying case in the other as we left the trailer and headed down the knob. I was a homeless person about to hit the lottery, or at least that's what I hoped. I wished my father was here to see me become the next chapter in the Loomis Gang history.

As we reached the damp bog the smell was like rancid cabbage and there was a glowing white fog seeping from the edges of the eight-foot tall swamp grass. The cattails were swaying in the gentle breeze of what the Oneida Indians called the "Great Swamp," or "Skiwanis," with over 7,000 acres inhabited by what they believed to be evil spirits. Even the Oneidas knew to stay out of there.

We were walking at a quick pace, single file, hanging onto each other's ropes like circus elephants on parade, when we saw flashlights coming up the hill behind us.

"Pick up the pace. We're being followed," yelled Shane. Snider was limping but was able to keep up with our near run. Shane ducked under some brush that looked like an impregnable wall until we got on the other side and found there was a path. The white glow of the gibbous moon lit our way. I could hear yelling behind us and realized that whoever was following us was getting really close.

We ran over some wet planks that were laid across blackened water or mud, I couldn't tell, when Snider, who was bringing up the rear, slipped and landed next to a plank. We halted and Shane jumped around me and grabbed the grass cutter by the shoulders, pulling him back up out of the swamp water. Once we got across, we pulled the planks free and hid them in the underbrush.

The flashlights stopped abruptly at the edge of the wetness, a beam of light hit my face. Whoever was following us quickly retreated and hurried to make their way around the far side of the swamp and back to the path we were taking. I could hear the group yelling for us to stop, but we didn't look back. We came to a clearing and Shane stopped under a large oak tree that was alien in this land of sumacs and bullfrogs.

"Shhh. Everyone quiet," he whispered, as we sat in the moist grass. We had ducked under the branches which formed a protective canopy.

We suddenly heard a blood-curdling scream for help and we all knew the band following us was in big trouble.

"All of you stay here," ordered Shane. He dropped his gear and unhooked the rope. We all unburdened ourselves of the equipment, untied the ropes from each other, and stupidly followed our leader who had only a single flashlight. A few turns on the path and we stopped halted right behind Shane who stood on the edge of a black pool that reflected the moon and trees on its rippling surface. The steam rolling off the top smelled acrid. Shane shined his light and found several people struggling in quicksand.

"Please-help!" It was the voice of Lyndon Johnson. We scurried around to the spot where he had fallen in. The reporter was clinging to the tip of a tree branch that had bent down to the surface of the quagmire. He was desperately trying to pull himself free of the muck by climbing up the bent branch, but couldn't. We could see Kicker next to him, hanging onto a broken log that was barely keeping him up. He was as white as a ghost but was silent in his terror. I never remember him not opening his vulgar mouth, but potential death had silenced him.

The third person stuck in the muck had to be the mayor for the last thing we saw was his jeweled fingers grasping at the air. I recognized his championship ring glistening in the flashlight beam. The oily quicksand sealed over his fingers in seconds leaving nothing but his toupee sitting on the surface.

"I have a wife and child. Please don't leave me here to die," cried Lyndon Johnson.

Shane took a long stick and Kicker took hold. It took all of us yanking on the slippery wood to move him through the gooey mud. He struggled to get up, then quickly sprinted back out of Nine Mile Swamp like a possessed man.

I took the stick from Shane. "Stay back everyone," I directed as I circled the bog, slipping and sliding in my cowboy boots, trying to get as close to the obnoxious reporter as I could.

"Daisy, you'll never be able to pull him out by yourself," cautioned Shane.

"Stay back. Stay over there. I mean it!"

"Thank goodness its you. Please, hurry. My fingers are wet and cold and I'm losing my grip."

I swung the stick like a bat and whacked his knuckles so hard the wood cracked and the noise echoed into the misty darkness. The tree branch whooshed back up into the air from his release. I took the end of the stick and poked him in the head with it and pushed with all my might to make him go under quicker. There was yelling from across the muck, but I zoned out for all I could hear was the banshee screaming in my head.

I chuckled to myself as the loudmouth disappeared without uttering another pathetic sound. A final bubble appeared, then burst, allowing the last breath of the reporter to escape. I stood up and threw the stick as far into the quicksand as I could. No more women will be victims of an "incident" at the hands of Johnson. I shook the wet quicksand off my hands, then brushed the remainder of mud onto my pants, and adjusted my bent glasses.

"You crazy bitch," screamed Jessica. She looked at me with wide eyes, mouth agape. For once she was speechless and I was superior. I nodded my head.

"Let's move before anyone else comes after us," I barked.

"Amen," said Shane.

We returned to our gear, tied ourselves together again, with me at the end this time. We picked up our provisions, hearing only the sound of swamp gas hissing and millions of crickets rubbing their bony ankles together. Fireflies were drifting randomly about. Snider refused to look at me, walking with his face looking down, watching the path intently. We marched until we reached the clearing and set our tents up under the flashlight beams. Snider and I each had our own two-man red tents and Jessica and Shane stayed in the blue one.

The smell of the quicksand on my hands was foul so I reached out of the tent and finished wiping my hands clean on the wet grass. I took off my boots and my leather pants, setting my switchblade to the side. I then took off my shirt and bra and slipped the switchblade under my chunky foam pillow. I was naked inside the protection of my nylon cocoon listening to the continuous songs of the crickets. I loved sleeping naked as the day I had been born.

In the morning we would be making our descent to our riches. I opened the cat carrier and Doodle circled the interior of the tent howling out to any animal that would listen. I poured him a cup of water from my bottle and placed some pieces of Meow Mix on my sleeping bag that he drank and ate faster than usual, and then went back to howling. I eventually unzipped the door to let him prowl for the night. He would be back in the morning. He was old, but he still had his claws, a few teeth, and a nasty disposition. I knew my boy could handle himself.

I was wide awake, all pumped up about the library. I tapped a drumbeat on the bowler. It matched the sound of the bullfrogs croaking all around us. To honor my father, I decided to wear the hat down into the hole instead of the helmet. I had no job or home anymore so that gold had better be there or I'd be flipping burgers with a timer dinging in my ear. I'd probably have to beg Blanche to let me live with her. I didn't want to think of that horrible existence with Don coming home drunk every night sleeping on the floor in the bathroom blocking the toilet. I'd rather die in the cave than live that way.

I felt guilty about killing Lyndon Johnson, but in my mind I felt I had justification for the way he had treated me. Perhaps I saved others from the pain and humiliation of being violated by him. I'm sure his wife and kids will have some kind of insurance policy and she may be thrilled with him being gone. What's better for her, an egotistical jerk of a husband or five hundred thousand dollars in life insurance?

I couldn't imagine being married to that man. I'm sure the folks of Waterville will give me a medal since I relieved them of a real jerk. He sure seemed to lose his smugness when that mud filled his pompous mouth.

I snipped the tip off one of my cigarillos and clicked my zippo. I opened the tent a smidgen to exhale the smoke out into the night air.

I looked up to the sky and whispered, "Sorry, Father."

Chapter 23

The Bearded Lady

"The Bearded Lady" was the nickname I had given to one patron of the Waterville library. She was a woman in her fifties who wore clean pressed business suits, but had a few random catfish hairs beneath her chin. She would always talk really loudly into her cell phone annoying the other patrons who were trying to enjoy the intellectual serenity. She wore garish rings on her fingers, and had multiple baubles hanging from her wrists that jingled like Christmas bells when she'd emphasize a point. Worst of all she wore bright red lipstick that was always, and I mean always, on her teeth when she smiled. If it wasn't for the few hairs on her chin, she'd be breathtakingly beautiful with her emerald eyes and her long dancer's legs that always seemed to be glowing with oil in the dimly lit library. She looked like a model but it was impossible not to notice those hairs.

Daisy Daring

I heard someone coming towards my tent, so I clenched the cigar between my teeth, threw my bowler to the side, and felt under my pillow until I found my switchblade. I felt the handle, until my thumb rested on the release. Shane popped his head into my tent.

"Mind If I come in?"

"No problem." I pulled the covers up over my body. I picked up my cowboy boot and extinguished my cigar on the heel, leaving just the illumination from Shane's flashlight.

"Jessica's asleep and I wanted to talk to you." He sat and crossed his legs. He ran his fingers through his hair revealing his dark eyes and wrinkled brow. "I'm not going to judge you for what you did back there to Johnson. I know I blabbed to him at the Spit Pea. I'm sure you had your reason, but I can't promise Jessica will keep her mouth shut."

I looked down and realized that she just might turn me in for murdering the reporter. It would be just her style.

"I can't tell you why I did it right now, maybe someday I can. I didn't think I had it in me, but believe me I had my reasons. I just know I'll never murder again." I bit my lip until I tasted blood. I didn't want the truth to come out. I just sucked it up.

"I was really impressed with the way you deciphered the code on that skin. I never even heard of the Welsh, let alone of their language. It sure looked like gibberish to me."

"Well there's a good thirty dialects of Welsh, but my father happened to be educated on the local one that's been around for a while. Another Welsh speaking person might not have been able to completely translate it though." I did have help but he'll never know it. "I do wish my father were alive to see this. The Loomis Gang was his passion. He felt the gang never got the respect it deserved."

"Well, people around here seem to know us pretty well."

"No, I mean way beyond the boundaries of this place. Your ancestors controlled all of upstate New York to Canada, from Pennsylvania over to Vermont. With over two hundred members, it was the biggest family crime syndicate of the nineteenth century and besides, your family was educated, even the women. I loved hearing about Cornelia and her sisters. Women back in those days were not educated like today; they were treated like cattle. Not allowed to vote. Branded by roughnecks for breeding stock, but not so with the Loomis women. It's a fascinating story."

"My book will change all that when it comes out. Will you help me with it, Daisy?"

"I would be happy to. Your writing is so raw and passionate that no trained writer could duplicate it. Anyone can polish the rough edges, the grammar and such, but the passion behind it is what leaps off the page." I didn't want to hurt his feelings because his book was filled with misspellings and grammatical errors, but I saw through these faults to the real gem inside.

"I sort of came over to ask you to help me with my book. I have written some more and when we're done I want you to check it out. I don't know why Jessica thinks I'm such a dumb stump. You're smart and you liked it. But, I really came over because I heard your lighter, and I can't sleep. I'm just so excited about what we'll find tomorrow."

"She's jealous of you, Shane." I reached over and touched his hand. "You being better than her at things threatens her. I don't think she's the girl for you. I mean, you both have the same type of background, but you're, you're... different. Know what I mean?"

"Yeah, I think I do." He leaned in and kissed me and I felt fire up and down my spine. I had longed for this moment. It had been so long since I had made love. Even though I chose to be alone, I was still a woman who needed love. He slowly took off his shirt and climbed into my sleeping bag. We made wild passionate love and fell asleep in each other's arms.

When I woke up, Shane was gone and Doodle was sitting on my chest purring, stealing my breath like he used to do in the apartment. The sun was burning brightly and my red tent glowed in the morning light. I rolled over and opened the cat carrier and Doodle limped in and lay down. I don't know where he was gallivanting, but he must've had fun, for his gray and orange underside was stained black from the muck, turning him into a three-toned tabby.

I sipped some of my bottled water, wishing I had a toothbrush. My mouth felt dry and pasty. I wondered if Napoleoni had doubled back and started the fire or perhaps it was the mayor, Kicker, or Lyndon Johnson.

I thought about being with Shane. If Jessica ever found out about us, I'm sure she'd do a lot more than knock the glasses off my face. I knew she'd probably kill me. I had a feeling she was going to try and get rid of me in any event. I vowed to make the first move if she dared try anything. After what I did to that reporter, I felt pretty invincible.

"Hey, egghead," yelled Jessica, from outside the tent. "Time to get up and have breakfast." She slapped her hand against the nylon.

"I'll be right out."

My leather pants felt stiff and cold when I pulled them on and the dried black quicksand crumbled off as I yanked them over my hips. My boots were covered with the same gook and I wondered what the mayor had thought as he was pulled down under.

I unzipped the tent and went out into the sun, and rubbed my arms. It wasn't hot yet, but it was going to be. Snider, Shane, and Jessica were sitting on the ground eating power bars and drinking Pepsi out of a liter bottle that they passed around. I sat next to Snider and took my turn with the communal drink that I spit out when the fizz went up my throat the wrong way and bubbled out my nostrils.

"We can't have any campfires, in case someone comes in looking for the mayor. They'll trace our smoke," said Shane. He flipped his hair back and gave me a little smirk that made me feel uneasy.

Jessica glared at me while we finished our meal, with me looking down at the crushed bed of grass that was drying fast in the morning sun. We packed up our gear and followed Shane, looking for the place where the upside down horseshoe was nailed to the tree. He went with Snider into the woods to scout something out, leaving me alone with Jessica.

"He's using you," she gloated.

"I don't know what you're talking about."

"You're naïve for a chick. You think the tooth fairy visited you last night? He's slick and you don't even see it." She placed a stick of chewing gum in her mouth, crumpled the wrapper, and tossed it into the long grass. "When this is all over, he'll keep all the gold and I'm going to choke you."

"You can't threaten me."

"Why? You think pushing some man down in the mud makes you tough? I'll slap you to the floor like I did before, you better believe it."

"You can't find the gold without me."

"Your blackmail is over. We're out here now and you'll show us or Shane will leave you out here to rot and you'll never find your way out."

I felt the blood leave my face for I knew she was right. Shane had gotten the best of me and now I had no escape from here. That's probably why they shrugged off my murdering Johnson. I felt like such a fool. I could hear Blanche and Don laughing at me. I needed that gold to build my library and get my revenge on them.

I saw something out of the corner of my eye and turned to see a monarch butterfly land on my shoulder. It stretched its orange and black wings and took flight once it was warmed up. I couldn't help but smile at nature placing such beauty in such an ugly place.

The men came out of the patch of woods laughing at something, with Shane patting Snider on the back. I didn't understand why men had their own language. They seemed to prefer the company of other men, where us ladies prefer to be on our men's hips every second, not liking other females around, except maybe our daughters or mothers. Well, not if they have a Blanche for a mother.

Suddenly there was a loud whirring heading our way.

"Into the brush and hurry!" yelled Shane. He was waving his arm at us as we ran with all of our equipment into the protection of some tall swamp grass.

A blue and yellow New York State Police helicopter whirred overhead and then disappeared over the distant tree line.

"They're looking for the mayor and that reporter," said Shane.

"Must be Kicker got back to town. Probably cried all the way before calling the police," laughed Jessica.

Shane silently tied us all together. He became stern. "You saw what happened last night to foolish people who venture into the Nine Mile Swamp. You march single file behind me, no straying off the path. If one of us goes under the rest can pull them out."

"Unless Daisy helps you," snickered Jessica.

After we had marched for a while I looked back at the tall grass thinking we were leaving a broken, trampled trail for others to follow, but to my amazement, the swamp grass was billowing back up erasing our existence.

"You said one hundred rods to the upside down horseshoe?"

"That's right," I answered.

"I think I know where the horseshoe is," said Shane.

We halted at a creek that seemed too wide for us to jump with all this gear. I set Doodle down and my puss seemed to be handling the cage a little better than last night. He was still meowing but it wasn't the scared howling of earlier.

Shane untied himself and told us not to move. He came back a few minutes later with a twelve-foot plank and laid it across the creek to the other bank. He repeated this twice with planks each about a foot wide, it gave us a nice bridge to walk over. I remembered my father saying how the Loomis Gang had used this trick to bring their stolen horses deep into Nine Mile Swamp until they were ready to move them down to New York City.

Shane tied himself back up and led us over the boards. The old planks creaked as we walked across. I was scared they were going to snap at any second. I honestly don't know how they held us up. If the planks had cracked, we would've drowned with our corpses bound together for eternity. It's a good thing nobody on this expedition was very heavy or we'd have been in the drink.

As we crossed, I looked down at my reflection in the dark water flowing beneath us and wondered what creature was spawned in this primordial soup. The first air breathing creature probably slithered out of this bog a billion years ago and his direct descendent probably still lived here.

Once we were across, Shane untied himself and pulled the planks out and shoved them into the tall grass. We headed to the horseshoe nailed to the tree.

"I had been here once as a kid, but I left the horseshoe figuring it had some kind of importance," said Shane. "All right Daisy. Where do we go now?"

"The skin said to go twenty rods north to a large flat field where they hid their horses. We have to go to the south end of the field by a large boulder." I knew we were close to where the hole was at the edge of the field. "Once we get closer, I'll let you know just where it is."

We were marching when we heard a screech that caused us all to stop and look up. A hawk was dodging two crows that were cawing and pecking at it, trying to get it to leave their territory.

It was getting really hot really fast. It was sure to be a ninety-degree day and the stench of the bubbling swamp burned my nostrils. The bog was black as coal and I had to stop every so often to scrape thick muck off the bottoms of my cowboy boots.

We got to the field and there were still some remnants of the horse pens that the Loomis Gang had erected over a hundred years earlier. This had to be the hidden meadow that Wash and Grove had used to hide their stolen horses in. My father would have been ecstatic to see this. We halted next to some fallen posts. I rubbed my hands across them with wonderment and got a sliver. I yelped and sucked my finger.

"Why don't you marry it," taunted Jessica. She was sneering at me. "They're just stupid wooden posts. Damn crappy fallen fence built by criminals."

I looked at Snider, who was grinning. He agreed with me without having to say anything.

"There should be a small hole by a big rock down at the edge of the south end. Wash described it as about three feet across, and fringed by long grass that almost covers it completely. They found it when their dog fell in," I explained.

"Alright. We'll have to stay tied together until we find that hole," decided Shane as we marched across the damp grass. "In case one person falls in, we can keep them safe."

Shane headed for the south end of the field and picked up a branch with no bark on it that had to have been left there by the Loomis Gang, for none of the trees were large enough or close enough to shed such a large limb. I adjusted my crooked glasses while we were stopped and took off my bowler and wiped the sweat from my forehead and from the back of my neck with my dry fingers.

Shane used the stick to poke the ground in front of him before each step to make sure he didn't fall into a hole. I counted two hundred steps before we finally stopped at the edge of the field. He looked to the left and the right and went to his right. A few steps later he held up his hand near a large rock.

Shane dropped the stick and his gear bag, and untied himself. "This is it. Be very careful." He got down on both knees and began feeling around. He found a soft spot and pulled the grass away, exposing a hole the size of a manhole cover. He picked up a pebble out of the dirt and threw it down. We couldn't hear it hit the bottom.

Chapter 24

Harry Daring

When I was twelve years old my father had brought me to visit Loomis knob during my summer vacation. We had a picnic lunch next to the obelisk. We sat on Blanche's favorite black and white checkered tablecloth, eating crunchy peanut butter and strawberry preserve sandwiches, and shiny green apples. We shared a jug of sun-brewed tea with slices of lemon. The best part was the dessert, plumb pudding wrapped in tin foil.

"This is where they operated from," my father had told me. "The Loomis Gang used this hill to their advantage. They could see Filkins and his posse coming and they would rush into the Nine Mile Swamp over there. Nobody would dare follow them, concerned for their own fate. That's why the gang hid the stolen horses in the swamp. And that's why they hid their fortune in there. A few brave souls have gone in to find it and have never come out. It's very mysterious in there. One of these days, little darlin', I'll let you in on the secret." My father was tapping his bowler and nodding his head.

I liked it up there. I could see all the way to our house. I took a bite from my sandwich, and rubbed the gritty strawberry seeds against the roof of my mouth. A bee had zoned in on the scent of our sweets, so I waved him away. My father loved nature and pointed out the various trees that were in the swamp: pine, cedar, hemlock, and balsam. I loved walking along the edge of the swamp, dipping in just far enough to see a blue heron sail overhead or have a frosted elfin butterfly land on my hand.

"Where did the Loomis family go?"

"Honey, they were driven back to New England by Filkins and the Civil War vigilantes. Once the hardened veterans of the war came home, the locals were less afraid." My father looked around as if a gang member on horseback would appear at any moment. "Those veterans fought with muskets, bayonets, and their bare hands. You think a few thieves on horses scared them?"

"No?"

"Hell no, Daisy. Those men were like ghosts. Nothing but empty shells wandering home in blood soaked uniforms with fear erased from their existence by God."

I took a sip of my cold iced tea and clinched my jaw, for the cold had shot pain into my cavity.

Shane Loomis

We froze when we heard the helicopter, but it never came over the trees. It was hovering near the quicksand where the mayor and Lyndon slumbered. I was worried that I might be the next victim with Jessica and Shane disposing of Snider and myself once we got the gold. After last night, he seemed quiet and cold towards me. I thought for sure he'd get rid of Jessica but there he is, down on one knee, helping take her gear out of its bag.

I took out my white helmet that's cracked like an over-boiled egg, and threw it aside. I stretched the headband flashlight over my father's bowler, clicking it on to be sure that it worked. I stopped what I was doing to open the pet carrier and console Doodle. He wasn't looking particularly well. I probably should have left him back at the trailer but I was worried about him being abused or cooked alive in a trailer fire, roasted like my ark. I vowed that once I got my share, I'd go right back to starting a new ark. I'll carve all the dead animals and so many new ones that the ark animals will bulge at the seams.

I checked my boot to be sure the switchblade was still with me in case I needed to defend myself. I put on my harness and jumped up and down until my thighs felt snug in the looped black webbing. I picked up the blue carabiner hooks, looking at everyone, not knowing what to do next.

"All right, Snider. What do we do now?" asked Jessica.

Snider stepped forward, mumbling, and started tying what he called the "alpine harness" to my rope and through a couple of the carbiners. Next he anchored another rope to an old oak tree that must have been used by the Loomis Gang, for the cortex was rubbed away leaving a scar around the trunk. The rock by the hole was large and smooth and not a good anchor. Snider took out a funky looking ratchet that he called a "shunt" and snapped it onto the rope.

He stopped us and said, "Remember not to get anxious and go too fast when abseiling down or the rope will melt."

"What the hell is that?" Jessica sneered.

"Ummm, descending down into the hole," replied Snider. He was looking down at the knot he was tying. "We have to determine the depth of this hole because the rope has to hit bottom or you'll fall off the end and plunge to your death."

"I got you covered, big guy," Shane was talking to Doodle. He had tied one of the ropes to the carrying case and was walking towards the sinkhole.

"You can't do that," I screamed, frantically, as Doodle shrieked as he was plunged into the darkness. Suddenly I felt a thump on the back of my neck. When I came to, I was face down in the tall swamp grass. It tasted like pickled straw. I felt around blindly for a minute until I found my eyeglasses underneath my leg. I rolled over and was seeing double and rubbed my eyes until they were back in focus. My poor glasses were bent back into yet another direction. My bowler had flown off and sat, dented, on the ground. I sat up to see Shane lowering the rope, with Jessica next to him. Snider had retreated behind a tree, and was picking bark off of it.

"Don't try anything or I'll crack your skull and throw your ass down this hole," Jessica threatened. I sat on my knees clenching my fists. I reached around and felt the moist knot on the back of my head. I pulled my wet hand back around, and saw blood. I wiped it on the grass. I wanted to take out my knife and plunge it into their throats for what they were doing to Doodle.

"Why?" I asked as I picked up my bowler and punched the dent out of it before placing it back on my head.

"This is an experiment," explained Shane. "It's just like the soldiers in the Great War, when they'd have birds in cages next to the trenches. If Tweety plopped dead, that meant there was mustard gas and you put on your gasmask or you were dead too, same thing here. We will know when this mangy thing gets back up if we had enough rope. And if he comes up okay, we know there's no poison gas down there."

I could only imagine the fear Doodle was experiencing, being plunged into the unknown abyss. His night vision eyes certainly would help him see, but still, this was cruel. At least we're going down willingly. It seemed like an eternity as Shane let the rope slip through his fingers a foot at a time before it finally went slack with about six feet to spare.

"Seems my ancestor was correct in estimating the depth of this hole," boasted Shane.

"Leave him down there for a few minutes before bringing him back up. Maybe he'll be a cooked little pussycat," laughed Jessica. She and Shane joined in making me feel foolish and ashamed for falling for him. They will pay for this.

"Bring him up now... please." I was on my knees, frantic about my boy.

Shane started to pull back up, slowly, trying to keep the rope from rubbing the rocky rim of the cave. I crossed my fingers Doodle wouldn't be dead, and I could hear the echo of his primitive howling long before the carrying case came back into the daylight.

"Well, looks like your pussycat made it out okay," said Shane.

I grabbed the carrier from the laughing duo and untied it while Doodle was scratching and howling to get out. I set down the cage, saying, "I'm sorry, puss puss, so sorry." I opened it and he sprinted into the long grass faster than I had ever seen the old boy move. I knelt down and crunched my fingernails deep into my soft palms.

Snider took the rope and slipped it through my harness and the hand cranking device, mumbling under his breath, while I adjusted the straps on my bowler.

"Now remember, Daisy, this device will lower you a few inches at a time. It's slow but very safe." He showed me how to crank the handle up and down letting the rope slide through. "You unhook yourself and walkie talkie up and we'll send the next person. We can have all three of you on the rope at the same time; it can handle the weight, but its not as safe."

Shane was cold as he handed me the walkie talkie and stepped a few feet away to test the signal. It worked, so I strapped it onto the harness and walked over to the hole, worried about what had frightened Doodle so much.

"Don't steal our gold," warned Jessica. Where did she think I was going to go with it?

"Now when all three of us get down there, Snider, I want you to send down the extra rope with the large duffle bag to carry the treasure back up to the surface," ordered Shane. He knelt down near the hole and waved me over. I could hear the whirr of the NYS police helicopter in the distance as I looked down into the hole and wondered if I'd meet the mayor in Hades.

Snider pulled the rope through the lowering device until it was tight. "Now, remember that you don't have to kick off the walls, but you can if you want. The Gringris works with only one rope, making it easier for beginners. This device is meant to lower and raise you back up with no support from the walls," Snider cautioned us.

I closed my eyes and prayed to my father to keep an eye on me. I had no choice, with no library, no job, and no man to support me. I could hear my heart beating wildly as I plunged down over the lip of the cave and exhaled deeply to relieve my stress as I hung over the abyss. I was a Troglodyte empress about to conquer my underworld kingdom. A couple snaps of the Gringris lowering device and I disappeared below the lip.

Chapter 25

Cornelia Loomis: The Loomis Gang 1865

After the burning to the ground of the Madison County Courthouse, and the return of the Civil War veterans, Sheriff Filkins and his team of vigilantes were rumored to be gaining members, making Cornelia more nervous then ever. Her brothers had gotten away with so much for so long they felt they were unstoppable. She knew better.

Wash and Grove had recently run a mission to steal a prized horse from Nathaniel Edwards down in Clinton and gotten unexpected resistance. John Browne, a newly arrived gang member from western Pennsylvania, went into a rage at the resistance and the result was that the old man was beaten to the ground. Nathaniel later died and yet the gang was still not worried about repercussions. They had made recent payments to all the local police, judges, and politicians, including extra ten-dollar bonuses.

The Loomis Gang were at the peak of their power, and they relished in their empire.

Cornelia sat in front of her bedroom mirror and brushed her wavy sable hair. She finished counting her two hundredth stroke, blew out the candle on her nightstand, and pulled the bedcovers back. She could see the half-moon out her window and traced it with her finger. She would fall asleep by herself. All these years of gang activity had left her without a husband, without children. She rubbed her flat stomach longing to have it bloat up with a baby. Jesse hadn't come back, yet she remained true to her word that no other man would possess her heart.

A loud whooping sound awakened the Outlaw Queen. She sat up and rubbed her eyes, pulled her robe off the bedpost and ran out of the room without a lit candle. Something was happening downstairs.

Cornelia's heart raced as she ran down the stairs, realizing the commotion was coming from the back of the house. The screaming and whooping grew louder as she got closer to the kitchen.

When she opened the kitchen door she was shocked to see white men with their shirts off painted to look like redskins. They were covered with either red paint or mud, with gray stripes painted under their eyes. She recognized the tall man as Filkins, who held what looked like a bloody muskrat pelt over his head and looked at her with angry bulging eyes. He waved a tomahawk. Then, as quickly as they had come, Filkins and his vigilantes bolted out the back door shrieking, leaving something behind on the kitchen floor.

The cold summer wind was blowing through the opened door that Cornelia slammed shut, before turning her attention to the lump on the floor. She stumbled around the dark kitchen, trying to find a match to light the candle on the counter. It was only when she knelt down with the candlestick in her hand that she realized the lump was a human being.

Blood was pouring from under the body, but she couldn't tell who it was because it was face down on the floor. She grabbed the shoulder and turned the body over, and gasped at the shiny white skullcap in the candlelight. Whoever this was, he had been scalped right down to the bone, blood was covering the face. She held her hand on his chest and detected no heartbeat. Cornelia grabbed a rag off the counter, knelt back down, and started wiping the blood off the face.

Cornelia gasped when she realized who it was. Wash had been killed by Filkins—the leader of the Loomis gang, murdered in his own home. Her premonition had come true. The Civil War vigilantes were gaining strength. She had the grim task of telling her mother that her beloved son, George Washington Loomis, Jr., had been killed by their worst enemy.

Chapter 26

Daisy Daring

I was swaying on the rope, hitting the shaft of the cave that seemed to get a little wider with each click. I had descended a good twenty snaps when I looked up and saw only pitch black, except for a bright little hole with three heads peering over the edge. I felt like a troll. The flashlight attached to my hat kept flickering on and off, making me more than a little frightened about not being able to see where I was going.

I paused and looked down, tapping the side of my bowler until the flashlight came on—the walls below appeared to be moving. I adjusted my glasses and went back to clicking. I gave the movement no thought until I started smelling an ammonia-like odor and heard a low squeaking sound.

I brushed up against a black spackling of bats that suddenly exploded off the walls, engulfing me. I screamed and a bat flew directly into my face then fluttered off. I spit and covered my face as thousands of flying creatures flew out of Swiss cheese-like holes in the rock, squealing vengefully, causing me to cover my throbbing ears. Boy, I thought, I got pissed when someone disturbed my sleep. Wash had never mentioned this in his writing.

I looked up but the light from the small opening above was blocked by the escaping mammals with wings. The flapping was creating a wind and I was being pummeled by the creatures of the night flying into me, rushing past me; they were as afraid of me as I was of them.

After they were all gone, I took the walkie talkie off of my belt.

Shane was buzzing me.

"You okay down there?"

"Yes."

"Christ sakes. There must've been a million bats come screaming out of the hole. They went into the trees, so I doubt they're coming back. Can you see the bottom?"

I looked down into the dark. "No, not yet. I'll call when I touch down." I clipped the walkie talkie back onto my belt, rubbed my quivering hands together, and took a deep breath before going back to lowering myself.

I kept clicking away and noticed that the bottleneck was expanding until I couldn't see the neck of the cave any longer, which scared me. I was free-swinging in an open cave when the rope slipped through the Gringris device, causing me to slide only a few feet but seemed like a thousand. The device took hold again and the sudden stop snapped me like a puppet. I don't know what hurt more, my lower back from the sudden stop or my heart from shock.

It seemed like forever before my feet hit rock bottom. I unhooked myself and wanted to kiss the floor of the cave, but resisted the urge. I couldn't see even a tiny flicker of light creeping in from anywhere.

I unhooked my walkie talkie again. "I'm at the bottom." There was silence, and I wondered if they could hear me or if they were going to leave me down here, and I was worried the spirit of the Loomis Gang was still down here.

"Stay put. Don't move. We'll be down in a little while," replied Shane. That had made me feel much better. They didn't have to worry about me exploring. The light on my hat was flickering again and they had flashlights, so I wasn't about to wander off anywhere. For all I knew, I was on a shelf, and one step would throw me down into the depths of the earth.

I pushed my bowler back and adjusted my glasses that had slid down my nose. The cave had a trapped air smell to it like when you go into your attic for the first time in a decade to get Aunt Ethel's wedding dress and all you breathe is hot dust.

I held my shaking hands to my leather-clad thighs and looked at the floor. It was covered with powdered sugar-like dust that poofed into little clouds when I tapped my boots on it. I crouched down, licked my finger, dipped it into the white fluff, then anointed myself by smearing the dust onto my forehead.

I heard some commotion above me, so I squinted upward, and saw a beam of light piercing the darkness coming from the mouth of the cave, which was about one-hundred feet above me.

Eventually Jessica was about twenty feet above and shouting out in the void. "Hello? You down here?" Her voice echoed off the walls and I instinctively put my forearm over my head waiting for the bats to reappear.

"I'm right below you. You're almost to the floor," I answered. I had to hit my bowler again to get the light to stay on.

Jessica landed and unhooked herself and let Shane know to come down.

"That was wild," she said. She was rubbing her hands together that must've been cramped like mine from the clicking device. "I thought those bats were freaky. I'm glad you went first."

"Yeah."

"You know, if we find the gold, Shane mentioned leaving you down here."

"Okay." I was trying not to let this bitch get to me. I rubbed my bare arms that had goose bumps from the rocky chill.

"I bet him he would never get you to sleep with him. Well, he won."

"That's a lie."

"It is, eh? I was right outside your tent when he was with you. You think he'd ever go for the likes of you? He doesn't like librarians, especially ones that dress weird. He used you and you don't even see it. He sucked you right in with his whole sensitive writer routine and you showed us where the gold is. Your cat ran off, your library is ash, and Shane will be taking care of your friend after we get outta here."

I looked up and could see Shane coming down from the miniscule entrance. I had promised myself that I would never be hoodwinked by another man after the Napoleoni fiasco. Now I felt ashamed and embarrassed.

I knelt down and looked at the dirt on the floor of the cave, when something caught my eye that I placed my palm over. I could feel it crawling beneath my hand and turned it over to see a glowing white millipede scurrying its thousand legs over my hand to get to the other side. I lifted my hand back up and the little bugger disappeared into the darkness. I thought of the Roman philosopher Seneca who hated caves and said to go into one was to "tempt the fires of hell."

Shane came down, unhooked himself from the device, and took my walkie talkie. "Alright Snider, we're down here. Send down the second rope and bag for the gold. Don't pull it back up until I give you the signal."

Shane took out a lithium powered miniature spotlight that pierced the darkness. He shone it up into the air, lighting up the vast interior that shone like a gigantic kaleidoscope. The roof was at least one hundred feet up, with our tiny entrance the only hole in the entire void. What really took our breath away was when he panned the light down the walls to the bottom of the cave to a black pool of still water. The underground lake was eerie and the lip of the water was only twenty feet in front of us. We could see footprints in the dirt that must have been left by the Loomis Gang over a hundred years ago.

"Wow," was all Shane could muster. The lake was a good thousand feet across and was surrounded by the cave so I couldn't understand how this water had gotten in here. There didn't appear to be a spring or creek flowing into or out of it. Maybe it just bubbled up from the bowels of the earth for it was as dark as bile. Shane picked up a chunk of the white powdered earth and threw it into the water, creating a splash that echoed like a musical chime in the trapped space.

He shined the flashlight at the floor and we discovered that we were standing on a raised platform of white powder that seemed to be guano. It was about twenty feet across and about two feet high. Along the dry side were white, pointed stalagmites sticking up in a row like hooded clansmen ready to pounce. Shane abruptly stopped the beam on a white ribcage sticking up into the air. We all walked a little closer and found the skeleton of a dog half- buried in bat crap.

"It's Jeb," I said, excitedly.

"Who?" asked Jessica.

"This here's Wash's prize pooch," said Shane. He handed the flashlight to Jessica and knelt down, rubbing his hands up and down the clean bones. "You know what this means?"

"Yes!" I shrieked, "That the gold's down here waiting for us.

Riches beyond our greatest expectations. The best of times."

"You got it," he agreed. He grabbed the flashlight back from Jessica.

Shane was slowly spinning around, shining the beam on the floor when we noticed a scraping mark towards the darkness, leading away from the lake. We followed it and found these pink flower-like shapes formed from the melting interior of the earth. I felt like I was walking on another planet. We spotted a pair of skeletal human legs sticking out from behind a large stalagmite. We walked around it and there was a former member of the Loomis Gang clutching a wooden strongbox by its metal handle, his mouth open in what appeared to be a frozen scream.

"It's Adam."

Chapter 27

The Politician

"The Politician" was the name I had given to one of the young male patrons of the Waterville Public Library. He was well-mannered, with a starched suit and bow tie that made him look like Orville Redenbacker's nephew. He'd shake my hand vigorously saying "Great job. Well done, well done," when I had finished checking out his book on the latest political movement.

The Politician would always have some kind of petition that he wanted me to sign like "Save the crossing guard" and "No more lima beans in the school cafeteria." He would walk around asking patrons what their views were and he'd take the opposite side just to strike up a debate. I was sure he was the future mayor so I always treated him with respect.

Jessica Suckling

"Who the hell's Adam?" asked Jessica, her annoying tone echoing around inside the chamber.

"That's what I named this poor soul. Wash never mentioned who this unknown victim of the Loomis Gang was, but every person deserves a name, so I named him Adam since he was the first down here."

"That's stupid," she glared at me.

Shane handed me the flashlight and knelt down and moved the skeleton off of the brown wooden box. He had to unlatch the lid before flipping it open. We all leaned in and the beam of light hit the gold rocks that filled the chest. It glowed, oh how it glowed! We were all in shock at the amount of gold and the beauty of it. It was the first time since I met Jessica that she kept her mouth shut.

Shane picked up a handful of the solid gold rocks, smiling while Jessica and I reached out and rubbed our hands over the rough nuggets. He put them back in the box and carried it over to where we had landed. He tied the rope around the box three times and through the handle, leaving the duffle bag on the ground, and took out the walkie talkie.

"Snider. You can bring up the second rope now. And do it very slowly, very carefully. This box probably weighs a few hundred pounds. Call me when you have it up there."

"Ten four."

He clipped the walkie talkie onto his belt. "Is he strong enough to get this all the way up there?"

"He's a man who works with his hands for a living, so he definitely has the strength," I announced.

Shane took the flashlight back and we watched as the trunk slowly rose higher until it disappeared into the lighted hole above. Jessica leaned into Shane, whispering in his ear, and the both of them looked at me and snickered. I was worried they were going to throw me in the lake and leave me here with Jeb and Adam. I clenched my fist to prepare to fight to the death. I vowed not to go gently into the night. I wished I could whittle these two down to weasels and put them on a shelf.

The call came from Snider that he had the gold up on the surface so all we had to do was get ourselves out of this pit in one piece and we would become the nouveau riche of Waterville. I could see Jessica buying a pink house and decorating it with red velvet chairs, black satin silk-screened rock posters, and a suit of armor. I could see Shane sitting behind his oak, roll top desk, writing his masterpiece on the latest Dell laptop. I would finally get my private library, and poor Snider would still be in the shed or mowing the lawn. He was getting paid per diem and wasn't to share in the glory.

"I'm going up first," announced Jessica. "This place gives me the creeps. I'm afraid of being closed in; so I want out of here." Her acid-washed jeans looked even tighter with the harness digging into her rear end. We watched her click up the rope, continuing to talk, spiraling until the light from her helmet and the sputtering from her mouth were engulfed by the black.

"You go next," ordered Shane.

"Okay." I wouldn't look at him. I preferred to dig my name into the dirt. If I died, at least a future explorer that discovered my shattered bones will know what my name had been.

"You're acting strange. I thought you'd be more excited with us finding the treasure. My fortune. My empire."

I didn't say anything because his words were scary to me. It was all about himself. Snider called down to let us know Jessica was up there. I was worried they were going to cut the rope when I was halfway up and I was still angry with them for sending Doodle down here. I snapped onto the rope and cautiously began to click myself up, knowing what I had to do.

The light Shane held grew smaller with each click as the black bottleneck came closer. I just hoped the bats didn't come back as I passed their lair. I was starting to spin in circles in the void. I was feeling as if I were about to puke up my breakfast.

Finally, I was in the channel that led to the outside world. The top was getting closer. My heart leapt as I passed the nesting wall of bats, but my anticipation was wont because they weren't back. I was glad that I was almost out of there. I could see the blazing blue summer sky up above. I guess I was paranoid the whole time about Jessica and Shane. She was just playing the kind of head games with me that young girls specialize in.

When I got to the top I waited a second for someone to help me out, then yelled up. "Hey! Need some help here!"

I heard some noise but couldn't understand what was going on. Perhaps Kicker was back or maybe someone else. Then I heard screaming. I hoped the state police hadn't shown up to stop us.

I grabbed the edge and spit out some gravel that spilled into my mouth as I pulled myself out of the hole. I rolled over onto my back, relieved to be back on top of the crust of the earth. It took a second for my eyes to adjust to the bright daylight. Snider and Jessica were scuffling over by the tree my anchor rope was tied to. He was on the ground yelling for her to please stop, with his arms flailing about.

My hands shook as I quickly unhooked myself from my umbilical cord and ran over to see Snider covered with blood. Before I knew it, Jessica spun around and rammed a blade into my stomach, forcing all the air out of my lungs as the cold steel entered my flesh. My bowler fell to the ground.

"Die!" she screamed. Her angry spit sprayed into my face, leaving droplets on my crooked glasses. She twisted the knife, smiling; it felt like a hot poker in my stomach. My ribcage stopped the rotation as I picked up my left-behind helmet and swung it at her with all my might, smashing it against her skull. Her eyes rolled back into her head and she collapsed at my feet like a rag doll, leaving the knife bouncing up and down inside me. I grabbed the handle and pulled with all my might, then dropped the bloody implement on top of the unconscious bitch. Blood started seeping down my shirt and off my leather pants while I held the wound with my hands. I went over to Snider, who was sliced to ribbons and could barely speak with all the black liquid he was vomiting; green digestive fluid was oozing out of his stomach. His trembling face was ashen.

"I'm sorry, Daisy. She was going to kill you," he mumbled, as he fell back to the ground and died.

I quickly rummaged through Shane's bag and found a roll of duct tape and peeled a strand away with my teeth, taking my hands off my wound just long enough to tear away a makeshift bandage. The lack of pressure on the wound caused another gush of blood to run down my legs. I lifted my shirt and placed the tape over the gash, stopping the flow.

Jessica was beginning to move, so I ran over and kicked her head with my boot. I looked toward the hole and saw that the rope was tightened—Shane was coming up to finish me off.

I grabbed her hair and began pulling her across the grass. She came to and slapped my hand away. I fell, landing with my face over the lip of the cave. I could see light down in the hole. Shane was getting close. I rolled over and stood up facing the loud-mouthed white trash who suddenly was silent except for her grunting. I must've given her a concussion because she was weaving.

I threw off my glasses and put up my dukes ready to bare knuckle brawl. We circled around like a couple of square dancers before

Jessica launched her right fist to my jaw sending me onto my back. I rolled out of the way as she tried to kick me. That caused her to slip and she landed near the entrance to the cave. I went berserk. I moved in quickly punching her squarely in the jaw, propelling her backwards. She fell straight down into the cave without so much as a whimper. I reached into my cowboy boot, and took out my switchblade.

Chapter 28

Harry Daring

When I was sixteen years old, my father was served with divorce papers. That would end up being the moment I would point to as when Blanche destroyed my childhood innocence. I had just come home from school and my father was sitting on the edge of the couch with his glasses off, looking at the floor, running his hands through his hair, his bowler sitting on the side table. It was one of the few times I had ever seen him with that hat off.

I sat next to him and placed my hand on his knee. "What happened?"

"Daisy... honey." He put his glasses back on and put his hand on mine. "Your mother wants a divorce. I tried to talk her out of it, but it's no good. We'll have to find another place to live."

"What about Don?"

"Your mother wants to keep him. It's not that she doesn't want you; she just doesn't want me to be alone. Waterville is a small town, so we'll be close enough that you can see her anytime you want."

I hugged my father and went to pack everything I owned in the old suitcase that had belonged to my grandmother. It was blue with yellow flowers, and smelled like mothballs when I opened it. I found a charm bracelet made of fake gold with red and yellow plastic beads in the inside pocket. I was sure it wasn't worth anything or Blanche would've hocked it by now. I placed it on my wrist and held it in the sunbeam shining into my now empty bedroom, and marveled at the sparkling plastic.

The only things my father left with were his clothes, books, whittling set, and the animals he had begun to carve for the ark. Blanche personally checked every bag and our pockets to be sure we weren't stealing anything that she wanted. She told my father that it was all his fault because of his stupid habits. She reminded him that he had chosen my name from a girly calendar he saw hanging at the local Sunoco.

I asked my father what he saw in that woman in the first place. He looked up in the air past me, and said, "She was my Helen," with the look of love in his eyes that was still there until the day he died.

"Here take this," demanded Blanche. She handed him a jar of pickles. "I hate these so you can have 'em."

My father never said a mean word about Blanche. I did it for him, calling her a "selfish bitch," which caused him to snicker and blush. He lectured me to be a "lady with class," although I caught him chuckling every time I said it. Nothing ever felt so good. I had loved calling her that. She deserved it.

Daisy Daring

I leaned over the edge of the cave and saw Shane about twenty feet from the top. He must've seen Jessica whiz by and knew he was about to die for he groveled.

"Daisy... don't do it!" His voice echoed off the walls. "I don't know what happened. I'm not going to hurt you."

I started to cut the rope. I really wasn't a killer, but I wanted my library, and after all they were going to kill me. Besides Doodle was missing. The bastard should never have laid a hand upon my man. The nylon rope was tough and I furiously cut at it, all the while Shane was clicking like mad to get out before I finished the job. He was only about a foot from the top when the rope snapped. He lurched and was able to grab the sides, keeping himself up, but he couldn't climb. I looked down. He was shaking and had tears running down his cheeks.

"Please help me. Don't let me die."

I went over, dumped the gold out of the ancient crate, went over to the hole, and threw the wooden box down upon Shane's head. He fell silently into the abyss. I heard a faint thump when he hit the bottom.

I fell to my knees holding my stomach. I could hear the NYS police helicopter coming towards me and hounds baying in the distance. They were coming. Coming closer.

I grabbed my glasses, stood back up, and wobbled over towards Snider.

"They're gone, Snider. I took care of them. I had to murder them or it would've been me. I'm sorry I wasn't up here to protect you."

The deputies burst through the clearing with a pack of hounds on leashes, some carried shotguns. The helicopter stopped overhead and hovered. Then there was a handful of men in black and white suits waving the uniformed men away. Doodle came running out of the underbrush and jumped onto my bloody lap. He was shaking in fear, his head darting back and forth, hissing in defense of his wounded mother. I hugged my old snaggletooth tabby as a swarm of bats blotted out the sun, heading back into their hellhole. I blacked out.

Blanche Daring

I woke up in a hospital bed a few days later. My mouth was dry as cardboard. Blanche handed me a Dixie cup filled with water. I tried to sit up. A tight bandage around my midsection held fast. The pain was intense.

"Where...?"

"You're fortunate to be alive," said Blanche. "You lost a lot of blood and they had to repair your insides." I looked over and Don was sitting in the chair, slouched back, watching the Jerry Springer show that was blasting on the television in my room. "Donald, turn down that television."

"Mother, my name is Don—I'm not a Disney cartoon." He rolled his eyes and got up, reluctantly turning down the volume and flopping back into the blue fake leather hospital chair.

"You're at St. Thomas Hospital," she informed me. "The police had to airlift you out of there. You're lucky they found you at all. The police want to talk to you."

"Where's Doodle? Where's my gold?"

Blanche turned her head to the door. I had to get my glasses off the nightstand to see who it was. I placed my bent spectacles back on. Standing with his "Smokey the Bear" hat in his hand was Sheriff Leech. Glenn, the scumbag, slid in behind him to hear what he was going to say to me.

"Daisy, I need to ask you a few questions."

He pulled the chair up to my hospital bed, leaned in, ignoring the nasty stare of the nurses' aide who'd come in to take my temperature, then stormed back out. "What in the hell happened in that swamp? I want you to tell me the truth because the state police will want to talk to you."

"Well, the mayor and that reporter fell into quicksand trying to follow us in at night. We were able to save Kicker but he ran away. He didn't even want to help." I paused to pour another cup of water, holding the brown plastic pitcher with both of my shaking hands.

"Yes, we know that part. Kicker came racing into town looking like a madman. We had to have him write it down because he was delirious from being trapped in the quicksand. He still can't speak. And we're out there dredging the swamp right now."

I continued, "We went down into the cave to get the lost gold of the Loomis Gang. We found it and when I got back to the top Jessica had stabbed Snider." I took a sip of water and felt creepy at the eerie silence in the room. Blanche and brood were paying really close attention in order to get their slimy tentacles on my gold. "Then Jessica stabbed me in the stomach and that's the last I remember—I blacked out after that." I looked down at my blanket because I was a terrible liar.

"Well, Daisy, the state police are going to want to talk to you when you're better."

"What about my gold?"

Sheriff Leech snickered, thumbing the lip of his hat. "Well it wasn't real gold. It was fake."

"What?" piped in Blanche. Saying what I was thinking before I could verbalize it.

"Yeah it's pyrite—fools gold."

"That can't be true," I cried. I was in shock.

"I'm afraid it is. The state took the rocks, just worthless chunks of dirt, nobody wants it. Seems Wash played you the fool little lady.

You know he was famous for his pranks."

I looked down at my hands that were pale and getting wrinkled. I didn't know what I was going to do now with no library, no job, no home, and now no money. All I had were my bloody clothes in a bag. Even my father's pocket watch was missing. I still had the faded bowler, now blood-stained, sitting on my nightstand. I could pick it up and still smell my fathers Aqua Velva.

"Daisy, we have to go," announced Blanche. She picked up her purse, fixed the lipstick in her mirrored compact. "I better feed Don or he'll be cranky all afternoon." Glenn had already left and Don and my mother soon followed. Sheriff Leech stayed and sat next to my bed.

"Daisy, honey, they're going to grill you, you know that?"

I nodded my head.

"I can be there with you if you'd like. I always loved your father. He was a decent man. Nobody in town could understand why he'd strap himself to such a bad woman," he said. He had caught himself being candid. "Oh, I'm sorry about that."

"Don't be."

"These state police detectives want answers. They pulled two dead people out of that hole in the ground, one dead man up above, and two missing community leaders sucked into the earth."

"But I didn't kill anybody."

"I know, but they'll want to give you a polygraph."

I did feel kinda bad about what I did to Shane and Jessica, but not Lyndon Johnson. Waterville deserved better than that jerk and so did I.

Sheriff Leech seemed to be back to the sweet and jolly man I remembered. It was the stupid allure of the Loomis Gang gold that had put a spell on him. I completely understood.

"You're off the hook with the library. The fire was ruled accidental because of faulty wiring, although everyone in town is convinced that Shane Loomis did it. You know how the Loomis' loved arson; anyway, you shouldn't have hung around with him."

I just nodded my head and planted my chin on my chest. The pain was getting intense and I was clicking the nurse call button on my bed to get a shot of morphine. I didn't know how I was going to pay for this visit.

"I have to go now but I'll be back to see you," promised Leech.

He leaned over and kissed me on the forehead. He looked like Santa with his white hair and granny glasses on the tip of his nose. I loved his accent. Even though he wasn't Italian, he had that east Utica twang that's so enduring. He put his hat on and was almost to the door before I stopped him.

"Where's Doodle?"

"Who?"

"My kitty cat. He was with me when I lost consciousness."

"Daisy, we didn't find any cat."

Chapter 29

Daisy Daring

It was a good week before I was able to leave the hospital; I was wheeled out by a nurse, because nobody was there to pick me up. The New York State Police had left me alone but I knew they were eventually going to grill me about what happened. I had called the Mother Mary's Shelter for women in Utica to see if I could stay with them. They had a closet-sized room for fifty dollars a month that had no door. It was cozy and safe and the staff was sweet to me. I got a part-time job working at the Utica Public Library as an aide, which meant I would have to do the tedious chores for the real librarians, such as organizing the massive amount of returns and dusting the bookshelves. It was a beautiful old library; and it was right on Genesee Street.

I hadn't heard from Blanche since she and Don left the hospital to eat that day. In all actuality, I hadn't heard from anyone from Waterville. I heard all the patrons of the Waterville Library now went to Clinton for their books.

I thought about Napoleoni laughing his ass off at all of the fuss and muss we had made about worthless golden rocks and that Shane, the man who had assaulted him, was dead. Shane had always marveled at his immortality, explaining to me that he'd been "tagged" by God, to live forever. While tens of thousands a day keeled over, he'd still walked the earth. Heck, for all I knew, he was immortal.

When I had saved up a few dollars, I spent my time visiting the pawnshops of downtown Utica, looking for my father's missing pocket watch. It wasn't even real gold. It was fake as well, but to me, the trinket was priceless. I had visited all of the shops except the slimiest one over on Bleecker Street called "Trinkets and Trunks."

The outside of the building was peeling, revealing several layers of yellow, red, and green paint from years of owners trying to brighten up the big, ugly brick building.

There were vacant lots on both sides where arsonists had burnt the adjacent buildings down. The lots were littered with crumpled newspapers, broken liquor bottles, and all sorts of trash. An old Ford pickup was slumped down on its flat tires, rusting back into the earth. There was an old bed, some bent aluminum siding, and an abandoned lawn chair.

The two men outside were smoking non-filtered cigarettes and passing back and forth a paper bag that held an anonymous alcoholic beverage. "Hey, baby. What's happenin'?" they said in unison as I walked past.

An overpowering odor attacked my nostrils as soon as I opened the front door that seemed too heavy for its creaking hinges. The smell was rancid, not unlike mold or rotting garbage. The cowbell on the door clanged, letting the owner know someone was entering.

The aisle was crooked and narrow and would never allow a shopper in a wheelchair to enter. I glanced at the stuff that I wouldn't take for free, let alone pay anyone a nickel for. There were piles of cracked wooden picture frames, bent baby carriages, and an assortment of scratched and dented furniture piled up to the ceiling. The glass display cases were filled with cheap gold jewelry, plastic beads, and a huge assortment of rock and roll pins and patches.

I dinged the bell on the counter because the sign next to it said, "ding" for service.

The owner came out and I was floored at his suave appearance. He was tall and thin, with his jet black hair slicked back. He had a pencil-thin mustache and he was wearing a neatly pressed three-piece navy blue pinstripe suit with a red tie and a matching handkerchief sticking out of the breast pocket. The outfit was worth more than the entire cockroach nest and its contents put together.

"Good afternoon," he pleasantly greeted behind his teeth that were perfectly straight and white.

"I'm looking for a pocket watch, one that came in here recently.

I had mine stolen and this is the last pawnshop in Utica."

"Ma'am. I assure you that I, for one, do not solicit stolen items."

"I'm sorry... uhmmm."

"No need to apologize." He held his hand up for me to stop talking, like he was a traffic cop. "Let me go in the back and see what I have. Please excuse me."

I heard a squeal, causing me to turn around and look at the floor where a large brown rat was sitting on its haunches waving its little front feet at me like it was a trained pet. It hid away when the owner returned carrying a Tupperware tub filled with pocket watches.

"Take your time and see if you can find the watch you're looking for in here." He clasped his hands behind his back and took one step back. I noticed he had one blue eye and one brown one. His angular cheekbones seemed carved of granite.

"Thank you."

It didn't take me long to find my father's watch. My heart raced as I rubbed my thumb across the worn knob. I opened it and it was still stuck on three thirty, just like it had been since my father had passed away and it was given to me. I wound it out of habit. I always figured I'd let him fix it when he returned from the grave, or his spirit would let me know when it was okay to correct the time. And, besides, it was always correct at least twice every day.

"This is it. This is the one. How much?"

"One hundred dollars."

I couldn't believe he said that with a straight face.

"You got to be kidding me! I can buy a new one for less than that. It's not even real gold or anything."

"The price is the price, ma'am. I did have someone in here yesterday admiring that very piece." He pointed his crooked jeweled finger at it making me wonder how many other peoples' heirlooms he was sporting on his fingers. All shiny and gaudy, a ring on every finger, with the largest diamond on his left pinky. "I could hold the pocket watch for you if you provide a deposit." He cracked a grin.

"I'll take it." I took the wad of cash out of my front pocket, peeled off five twenty dollar bills and threw them on the counter.

"It's been a pleasure doing business with you, miss." He snickered.

I walked out of there with the watch gently cradled between my two palms like an infant bird with undersized wings.

I stopped outside and rubbed my stomach that seemed to have gotten bloated in the last few weeks, I was wondering if my wound had caused a blockage or buildup of some kind in my gut.

Daisy Daring

Because I had to pay so much for the watch, I had to work at the Utica library for a few more months before I had the extra cash to pay for a taxi ride out to Waterville. I was getting threatening bills from the hospital for my care, but I didn't have ten thousand dollars to send them and I didn't have health insurance. I didn't even have the money for an interest payment and they were threatening legal action.

Before calling a taxi, I sat in the community bathroom at the Mother Mary's Shelter and removed the yellowing tape and gauze from my midsection. My painkillers and antibiotics had run out, as had everyone in my life, except Sheriff Leech, who accompanied me to the New York State Police and helped me defeat the polygraph test. He had given me a trick to use to beat the machine and it worked to perfection. I couldn't help but think of Napoleoni and if he read about what happened to me. I heard my little escapade was making national news.

I knew that there still must be gold hidden somewhere in that swamp. Wash had been a joker and my father had mentioned a map, but I decided that it couldn't have been the one Shane had found.

I had no health insurance, no cash, so I had to take care of myself from here on. The scar across my belly was bulbous red and raised, jagged, just above my belly button. I took out some rusty tweezers from the medicine cabinet that had nothing else in it, except an expired box of iodine wipes and a roll of silk tape, and used them to remove the rotting stitches that held my entrails in place. I cut and pulled one at a time, and placed them on the edge of the sink, repeating the procedure ten times until all the strings were lined up in a row. The sutures left tiny holes on my belly.

My nose ring was missing. At least that hole was intentional, I couldn't prove it, but I think someone stole it from me when I was in the hospital. I guess it didn't really matter because the cheap gold-plated trinket had begun to turn green. I'm surprised those vultures in the hospital didn't take my hair and organs as well.

I had to replace my destroyed leather pants with some stretchy waisted sweatpants that I bought for a dollar at the Salvation Army next door. Besides, my stomach had been getting even more bloated in the last few months and I couldn't button my leather ones anymore. This, in addition to the fact that I hadn't had my period in several months, made me wonder if my getting stabbed was the reason, or perhaps with myself being close to thirty, I was going through very early menopause. No, I was too young for that. The most likely culprit—Shane. I didn't go to the doctor because I still owed the hospital so much money.

Heather Simms

I heard the *Crabtree Courier* had replaced the missing Lyndon Johnson with a young girl, Heather Simms, who was barely out of high school. I was told she had tried to interview me when I was in the hospital, but I had been asleep at the time. That was the beginning of my achieving some kind of celebrity.

I bummed a ride to a lawyers office for a free consultation and I was told that even if the nuggets were real, I couldn't keep them since they were found on state property. The lawyer had told me we were lucky to not be charged with trespassing. Shane only owned the plot his trailer was sitting on and that's where I was heading.

I sat in the back of an old yellow taxi that had dented fenders that were rusty with age, and a short, elderly driver who could barely see over the steering wheel. He had the radio tuned to classical music and was more concerned with conducting his orchestra than paying attention to the road, which made me really nervous.

I had been working and living in Utica since I had gotten out of the hospital, and didn't notice the advancing Mother Nature of the fall, with her rotting fallen leaves and flattened dead flowers. The dramatic change from bright green to dull brown never ceased to enthrall me. I didn't know why, but fall was my favorite season.

Perhaps because I saw it as a time to prepare for some sort of rebirth, or something corny like that. I always wondered why we couldn't shed our old wrinkled skin and gray hairs and then become reborn in the spring. Mother Nature was cruel.

I could see Loomis knob a good ten miles away as we snaked through the back roads of Waterville. I understood why the Loomis Gang chose the pinnacle with its strategic view of the surrounding countryside. They had ample time to scramble down into the Nine Mile Swamp when they needed to.

I had the cab driver pull up to Shane's trailer and wait for me, with the vehicle running, since I only planned on staying for a few minutes. I was looking over my shoulder the whole trip to be sure there was nobody following, thinking that I might have more gold hidden up there.

All the windows of Shane's trailer had been smashed and the door was torn off its hinges and lay flat on the ground, with muddy footprints all over it. I walked around the back towards the woods.

"Doodle! Here puss! Here puss!" I held my hand up to my mouth like those Swiss yodelers. "Kitty, kitty, kitty!" I waited a few minutes and no Doodle. I had convinced myself my old friend would come out of the woods and jump into my arms. Perhaps he was meant to be free.

I stepped inside Shane's trailer and the place was completely empty; all the paper-thin kitchen cabinet doors had been kicked in and the walls were torn apart. It looked like the gold-fevered residents of the area had gotten over their fear of the Loomis', as the sole survivor of the gang was now dead. Evidently, even Wash's wandering ghost wasn't enough to keep treasure hunters at bay. If there was a map hidden in this tin box of a house, they sure would've found it by now.

There were papers scattered all over the floors and I recognized the canary-yellow lined pages right away—Shane's manuscript. I spent several minutes picking up the wrinkled yellow sheets. The looters had no idea that this was the real gold.

Chapter 30

Cornelia Loomis: The Loomis Gang 1866

After the murder of Wash Loomis, the gang became even more bold and dangerous. With the patriarch no longer there to quell the bloodthirsty Grove, Cornelia feared it was a matter of time before Filkins and his vigilantes returned to the knob.

"Mother, Wash's murder was just the beginning. Filkins and his vigilantes won't stop," she cried, standing on the front porch watching the sun turn the horizon and edge of sky a glowing blood red.

"Cornelia, we can't let these damn farmers think they got the best of us. You're a Loomis. You come from better stock. Just like the best horses we steal, we are the best people."

Just then, Cornelia spotted Grove running up the hill towards the house. He was carrying a fur coat in his hand and his eyes were wide open and wild. He said nothing, but limped around the corner of the house, blood running down the back of his thigh.

A sudden thundering noise caused Cornelia and her mother to look up. They saw Filkins and some fifty men approaching on horseback, all carrying rifles and torches. One of the men in the back had a length of rope with a hangman's noose tied in it.

Half the herd of vigilantes went down towards the Nine Mile Swamp to cut Grove's escape route off, forcing him to scramble inside the house. He hid in one of the many false walls the gang had constructed just in case they ever needed them.

Cornelia stood in front of the men as they dismounted.

"He didn't make it down into the swamp, sir," said a man coming around the corner.

"He's in the house then," said Filkins. "Move aside Cornelia."

The Outlaw Queen and the rest of the Loomis women huddled together as a man with an ax stepped forward and motioned the others to come inside. After about an hour of furiously chopping down walls, the men came back outside with Grove, his hands tied behind his back.

"We found him hidden in the wall upstairs," yelled the man with the ax, holding it over his head.

The posse took Grove over to the large oak tree and slung the rope over the lowest, sturdiest branch. They lowered, then tightened the noose around his neck. Rhoda looked at the ground, while her youngest daughters stormed out of the house to save their big brother. Charlotte and Lucia had stopped due to the raised arm of their sister Cornelia. They stood watching—upright, stoic, silent, proud.

Filkins stepped down from his horse. By dressing up like an Indian he had gotten away with the murder of Wash Loomis. But this was different, it was daytime and he was wearing his uniform and there were over fifty witnesses.

"Grove, confess to everything and give back Mrs. Jones' fur coat and we'll be lenient," promised Filkins. He wiped the sweat beads away from his eyes with the palm of his hand. Cornelia could smell the stench of the unwashed men, but refused to move her hand to pinch her nose.

Grove wouldn't say anything, so ten men walked backwards with the rope, forcing Grove to kick his legs in a desperate attempt to touch solid ground. His face turned blue and his body stopped moving so the men let him down and Filkins loosened the knot. He slapped Grove in the face and he snapped back to life.

"Tell us now."

Still no answer.

Filkins tightened the noose again and pointed to the sky, the vigilantes raised him up again; the outlaw's eyes bulged so badly they seemed ready to burst. They let Grove down again and this time Filkins had to throw a bucket of water on his face to revive him.

"Not going to talk, eh?"

Still no answer.

This time they pulled him up and tied the rope to the base of the tree, letting Grove kick until his face turned blue and a wet spot appeared in his crotch. His feet went limp and his boots fell off his feet, thumping to the ground.

The posse threw flaming torches onto the roof of the Loomis homestead. Cornelia and her mother Rhoda stood there, while Charlotte and Lucia kept running into the house to save possessions that the posse would then rip out of their hands and throw back in. Vigilantes circled the blazing house firing bullets into any gang member they saw.

The Loomis women fled Madison County with the few possessions that survived the fire, and headed back to New England, where they were wholeheartedly embraced back into the aristocracy and lauded for their bravery in such a savage frontier. Cornelia became something of a celebrity, and when she died, the title, "Outlaw Queen," was written on her granite headstone. She never was reunited with Jesse James.

Chapter 31

Daisy Daring

The last three years, after the fake gold fiasco, have been a fairy tale beginning with the birth of my one and only child, Buttercup Cornelia Loomis. Its weird being a celebrity with a best selling book, *The Biggest Fiasco: The Greatest Gang on Earth*. I took Shane's writing and used it as the backbone for a novel about the Loomis Gang, our whirlwind romance, and his murder by the dastardly Jessica Suckling, and the discovery of the fools gold. It ended with the birth of the last of the Loomis Gang bloodline. I got a publishing deal. My book soared to the top of the NY Times best-seller list. My readers never knew that the best writing in the book had been done by someone else. My editor sure had her suspicions. She said my writing was unusual in that it was brilliant in the descriptions of the Loomis Gang, but seemed watered down and lackluster in the rest of the story.

I made the big bucks when a Hollywood hotshot optioned the rights to turn it into a movie. I had no idea my life would ever take this path. Sometimes I felt I was outside my body watching the events unfold, as if in a dream.

And I finally achieved my lifelong dream. I purchased Loomis knob and built my library on the crest where the original Loomis homestead had been located. I built it next to Shane's trailer, which I kept so that Buttercup would never forget where she came from. I had it surrounded with a tall wooden fence. My library was a simple red brick Victorian-style mansion, with one large room that housed ten-foot tall bookshelves loaded with my favorite reading materials.

There was an antique stepladder to retrieve my next read. No science fiction was allowed in the Doodle Library.

Having a best-selling book, and making a wheelbarrow full of money was nothing compared to the birth of Buttercup. I loved having Blanche see what a real mother is like. She, Glenn, and Donald all sucked up to me in hopes that I'd include them in my good fortune.

Heather Simms

One day as I was leaving my library/house with Buttercup in tow, heading down to the Utica Craft and Hobby to get some whittling supplies, a woman came walking up the knob with a pad of paper in her hand and a pen behind her ear. She had short blonde hair with jet black roots and was wearing jeans and a black Rolling Stones t-shirt that looked to be about three sizes too small. I could see her white bra through the faded shirt.

"Ms. Daring?"

"Yes."

"I'm Heather Simms from the *Crabtree Courier*," she announced, and held out her hand for me to shake. I shook with my left because my right hand was busy gripping onto my little wild Buttercup, who'd run off with the wind if I let her go.

"Yes?"

I was wondering if I could interview you. You see, everyone is fascinated with your story especially after you made such a big splash with your book." She stopped talking and held her finger under her nose, which didn't stop a large sneeze from coming out. "Oh, I'm so sorry about that," she said with tears in her eyes.

I had avoided the press since my bad experience with the quest for the Loomis Gang gold, but that changed after my book and movie deals. Now that I had the cash and a smidgen of fame, they all wanted to be my buddy, to be my pal. At least with Blanche, Don, and Glenn skulking around I could keep my defenses on high alert, but everyone else alarmed me because I just wasn't good at reading peoples' motives. Sheriff Leech was the only one I trusted. He kept me out of jail and stopped by once in a while to say hello and give

Buttercup a lollypop. His gentleness reminded me of my father.

"Why don't you come inside? This way I can keep my eye on my daughter and I can answer your questions." She followed me into the foyer and I closed the solid oak door behind her. "Come into my reading room."

I held Buttercup by the hand and sat her at her little desk and handed her a coloring book. She was approaching three years old and loved scribbling with her crayons more than anything. She stuck her tongue out of the corner of her mouth when she concentrated. I fixed the yellow bow in her hair and pointed towards the red velvet high-back chair by the fireplace. "Please sit down."

I pulled up the other one, sat down, crossed my legs and waited for her to quiz away.

"This is a beautiful place you have here, Ms. Daring."

"You can call me Daisy. And thank you. Now what can I do for you?"

"I just wanted to do a profile on you and perhaps take a photo." She took out one of those tiny metal digital cameras with a Cyclops lens in the middle.

"You're such a recluse that everyone in town wants to know what you're up too?"

"Well, I'm attempting to write my next book. It's going okay except for that writer's block nonsense. I've been concentrating all my efforts on being a good mother to my little lady."

"I know what you mean."

"Would you like some lemonade? I made it myself," I offered, getting up from my chair.

"I want some, Mommy," begged Buttercup, right on my heels as always. She was so fast and silent, she sometimes scared me. I would lie in bed at night and sense that I was being watched and I'd open my eyes, and there'd she be right at eye level.

"Yes please, I would like some also."

I got up and poured the sweet yellow elixir into the green Depression glasses I'd bought at the Bouckville antique fair for thirty cents apiece. I cut and threw in a fresh lemon wedge. I also put in sugar, adding an extra spoonful for Buttercup.

"I read your book and I thought it was really interesting. The hunt for the gold was exciting; even though it turned out to be fake and all."

"Thank you."

"I was wondering if your library was going to be opened up to the public since the other one was burned to the ground by Shane Loomis?"

"I think it's wrong to blame him. Sheriff Leech told me the official ruling was because of faulty electrical wiring. And your answer in regards to this library is... no. This is my private library stocked with the books I like. I will decide who and when I'll allow anyone else to use the Doodle Library."

"Wasn't Doodle your cat?"

"And your point?"

"Well, the people in town—well, you know."

"No, I don't know. Why don't you explain it to me." I sipped on my frosty lemonade, glaring at the reporter over the edge of the glass, arching my eyebrow in that spaghetti western maneuver I'd been practicing in the mirror. The young girl began to stutter.

"I guess people think you're maybe a little strange and all."

"The interview is over. I have errands to run with my daughter." I got up and took away her drink before she had time for a sip, and opened the door. "Goodbye."

She walked out with her head down and muttering, "Weird witch." I shut the door on her as she turned to make a last point. I guess this won't help the sale of my next book.

"Mommy," said Buttercup. She patted her little hand on my jeans. "What does witch mean?"

"Sweetie," I replied, kneeling down, adjusting my new eyeglasses, "It was a term used by the Puritans to describe women so they could tie them to stakes and burn them alive."

"Okay." She skipped back over to her more serious work of coloring a teddy bear, within the lines, completely purple.

Chapter 32

Buttercup Cornelia Loomis

I picked out a brand new pair of leather pants for myself, in a blood red color and got Buttercup a smaller black pair at the Biker Blitz store in Whitestown. I knew Blanche would go nuts seeing her sweet little granddaughter in these and I chuckled as my little cutie pie spun in front of the mirror admiring her new "back cow pants" as she called them.

It felt good to have the extra cash to get new clothes. I was overjoyed that I could afford to buy new glasses as well. I did keep my old bent ones in my nightstand drawer, just so I wouldn't forget my previous life. The life of long ago when I was checking out the books at the Waterville Public Library. That reporter thought I should open the doors of my home/library. Maybe some day I'll let some of my favorite patrons from Waterville come; I'll have to think about it for a while.

Fat Agent Smith and Skinny Agent Jones

When Buttercup and I got back from shopping, a black sedan was parked next to my house making me more than a little nervous. A short fat man and a tall skinny one, both in black suits and white shirts, got out. They were wearing the same cheap aviator sunglasses I had seen at the dollar store. They took a step towards me and reached inside their jackets. I dropped my packages and pulled Buttercup behind me. My first thought was that the mayor's widow had hired these men to kill me.

"Ms. Daring?"

"Yes?"

"FBI." They pulled out their laminated identification badges at the same time, stepping forward so I could read the names—the skinny one read Jones and the chubby one read Smith.

"What is this some kind of joke?" I knelt down and hugged Buttercup, then picked her up off the ground, she kicked and squealed, but it kept her from bolting away. "What do you want?"

"This is in regards to the deaths of Lyndon Johnson, Jessica Suckling, and Shane Loomis," they answered in unison.

"The police questioned me and gave me a polygraph and I was cleared by the state. I had nothing to do with the deaths."

"We just want to take you to the Utica office, our Special Agent-in-Charge, wants to ask you a few questions. You're not being charged with anything, at least not yet." The round agent walked away from his partner and opened the back door to the sedan.

"I'm sorry, but I don't have anyone to watch my daughter on such short notice."

"I assure you it will be very quick and painless," answered Agent Jones. His smile revealed crooked, chipped teeth.

"You can bring your daughter ma'am. We'll bring you right back," promised Agent Smith.

I set Buttercup down because she was getting heavy. When I let go she ran and hopped into the front seat.

I ran over to the car, "Sweetheart. Get in the back seat with Mommy."

"No."

Agent Jones removed his cheap sunglasses, pointed to me, "Please."

I knew I should probably pick up the phone and call Sheriff Leech or an attorney. But, I got in and shut the door knowing this wouldn't be the first time my little girl wouldn't listen to me. I wanted her to be fierce and independent, but just not with me.

"Here you go, ma'am," said Agent Smith, handing my daughter over the seat like she was a sack of flour.

Jones put the sedan in gear and tore a dirt devil in my driveway that hung there till we were out of sight. I held my head down as we went through Waterville, for the nosey townsfolk would see me with these strangers and think something was up. I'm sure they were still pissed that Hollywood was going to film the movie based on my book down in the hills of North Carolina, away from unionized workers.

I was too concerned with my problems to pay attention to agents Abbott and Costello's banter. I held Buttercup's hand, getting more worried the closer to Utica we got because I had fooled the state police polygraph with the help of Sheriff Leech by using the old trick of taping a push pin in the toe of my shoe. All I had to do was grind my big toe into the sharp tip of the needle when the examiner asked me easy questions like "Is your name Daisy Daring?" and stuff like that. Sheriff Leech explained that the pain would cause my adrenaline to spike so when they asked me a question like, "Did you murder Shane Loomis?" I would hold off on pushing my toe into the tack and the spike of adrenaline would mirror the others, thus making a consistent reading.

I really wasn't afraid of going to jail because I had heard they have the best libraries tax money can buy. I was far more worried about Blanche taking over Buttercup and making her into a junior version of her chain smoking, cheap-suit wearing, slimy real estate self. At least I had my father alive to protect me from her, but my little baby would have nobody to shield her. The emotional scars would be irreversible by the time I got out of the clink.

We pulled up to a tall, gray building and I was escorted up wide granite steps that led to a brass and glass turnstile. Buttercup delighted in the rotating door and showed her joy by letting out a loud squeal that caused the front office government drones to jump. I was sure that innocence and spontaneity were probably not allowed in the bureau. The chubby agent walked in front of us and the skinny one in back. You'd think they thought that I was going to pull a gun and go on a Bonnie and Clyde spree with my toddler in hand.

The inside of the elevator smelled like stale bubble gum and the buttons had no numbers. I wondered if this was to confuse prisoners like myself. In spite of it all I was starting to regain my confidence. After all, I had been telling people the same story for so long, writing it down in my book, telling it on my national tour. Hell, in my mind it was true.

The large agent opened the door to a small generic room. "Please have a seat and our SAC will be right with you."

After they left, I pulled the gray metal chairs away from the small folding table. The walls, ceiling, and floor were all painted the same battleship gray as the chairs. There was a single light bulb overhead. There was the standard pane of double-sided glass on one wall, like the kind you always see on those television detective shows. Some gumshoe with stale coffee in hand was probably hidden behind it. There was a mounted camera with its red eye blinking, letting me know it was watching my every move.

The room smelled like sweat, and the light bulb was flickering. Buttercup had nothing to play with so she was strumming her little hands on the table to the peanut butter and jelly song.

Within minutes, a tall thin man with a gray flattop and bulging blue eyes came into the room carrying a brown envelope and a tape recorder, which he set down in the middle of the table. He was wearing the same generic suit and tie as the previous agents and had a neatly trimmed mustache.

"Nice to meet you, Ms. Daring. I'm Agent Harry Harrisson," he announced, holding out his badge. He placed it back in the inside pocket of his suit jacket. "I'm the special agent in charge of the Utica office." I shook his hand; it felt stiff and hard like a mannequin's. He had the same first name as my father. "Hi," he said to Buttercup. He got down on one knee to look her in the eye. She didn't say anything and looked to me.

"It's okay," I replied.

"Hi, Mister."

"Well, I'm sure you want to know why I brought you down here." He took a stack of papers out of the envelope. "I have proof that you murdered Shane Loomis and Jessica Suckling."

"I haven't done anything wrong and I was already cleared by the New York State Police." I felt around my shoe, pissed I hadn't time to place a tack in there. Hopefully, I wouldn't have to take another polygraph test."

"Just a moment," cautioned Harrisson. He got up from the table, and reached up and unplugged the camera making its red eye blacken. "There. We don't need documentation of our conversation, but I don't know if your little girl should be in here for this."

170

"I don't hide anything from her, besides I don't trust you government types." I picked up my daughter, placed her on my lap, and hugged her tightly.

"Ouch. That hurt."

He got up and opened the door to the interrogation room and waved a female agent over, who had a tight bun of hair with chopsticks holding her red Medusa curls in check.

"Agent Jane here will just take her to that desk over there... you have my word."

I loosened my grip and Buttercup sprinted out of the room. I don't care what this bulging eyed bureaucrat has to say, I won't knuckle under. Besides, I'm much tougher than the broad that got smacked around by Jessica.

"I didn't want your little girl to hear this."

"What do you want with me?"

"Your connections."

"What?"

Agent Harrisson took a pile of papers out of a manila envelope and pushed them over to me. I read the title on the top.

"Out of Ammo?" I flipped through the pages and realized it was a manuscript. "What am I supposed to do with this? I'm a librarian, not an editor." I was used to people coming in to see me, back when I ran the Waterville Public Library, with their badly written rabble expecting me to give them a writing career, thinking I had some inside information. Hell, back then I didn't know anyone in the publishing business, besides, I hated half of the books in that moldy old brick library.

"You have written a best seller, and you have Mary Vickaro as your agent, and I want you to highly recommend my book to her."

"What if it sucks? I can't compromise my integrity. Even if I like it, I doubt she'd sign you, she only represents non-fiction."

"Oh, she'll represent it all right because you have a little something called leverage. She needs you to write another book for her and you won't do it unless she takes me on as a client." He leaned back in his chair, smiling, clasping his hands behind his head, revealing yellow armpit stains on his wrinkled shirt. "I've been down this road before and I'm not screwing myself out of fame. Not this time. No way. No how."

"Sorry, but no." I put the papers back together and pushed them across the table, making the agent's smile disappear. "And nothing you can do or say will make me."

"Let me play something for you."

He pushed down the play button on the tape recorder and fiddled with the controls so that I could hear the crackling audio loud and clearly. It was my voice on tape.

Chapter 33

Agent Harry Harrisson

"They're gone Snider. I took care of them. I had to murder them or it would've been me. I'm sorry I wasn't up here to protect you."

Agent Harrisson shut the tape off. "Isn't that sweet?"

"I don't understand—how?"

"Simple enough. Your old friend wore a wire and a global positioning device for us. You see, he forgot to pay his taxes and was threatened with a stint in Otisville Correctional unless he cooperated." Harrisson stroked his chin and bobbed his head like an immature man who wins five bucks from a scratch-off lottery ticket.

I was shell-shocked; I didn't know what to do or say. I just sat looking at my opened hands on the table.

"That doesn't prove anything. I was delirious because I had just been stabbed." I could feel my heart pounding through my chest and my mouth was dry, like a large cotton ball had absorbed the moisture. "Can I have a drink of water?"

"Sure, I'll get it for you."

When Agent Harrisson opened the door, I looked around to see if Buttercup was okay, but I didn't see her. I worried what it would be like for her to not have a mother anymore. I had to fight this. I couldn't let this FBI hack put me away, banished to wear an orange jumpsuit for the rest of my life. I looked at the emerging liver spots on my hands that began appearing during my pregnancy, wondering how spotted and old my body would be when and if I got out of prison. I might end up in a nursing home penitentiary going from one hellhole to another with Blanche cackling from her perch with the other ravens down in hell.

Agent Harrisson came back into the room carrying a large pewter mug dripping with condensation that he put in front of me.

"Yes, okay, I will try to help you." I knew in my heart that if this writing were crap, I'd be in real trouble of losing my literary agent. Nobody knew, except me, that I plagiarized Shane on the first novel. Now I was writing my second one, and I was petrified because I didn't have an ounce of writing talent and I not only got a deal, I made big bucks off of it. Perhaps my reputation will sell the next one. Perhaps the buzz I created will help move it off the shelves. Perhaps I can write better than I realize, but I doubt it.

"Now that's what I'm talking about," he snickered, and stroked his mustache as I reached for his manuscript. "Read a few pages." He took the blue rubber band off the thick stack of crinkled paper, pushing the manuscript across the table.

"Okay."

"You know, I think it's really hilarious what happened to the mayor."

I looked up to see where he was going with this whole thing.

"I mean, how they found nothing but his hairpiece. Did you know that they dug for days but the slime kept oozing out of the swamp and filling the hole back in?"

"No. I didn't know that." That was a lie because I knew they never found the bodies.

"Yeah, yeah. They probed down a hundred feet and never found the mayor or that reporter. I heard they had nothing but the toupee in his coffin. That's pretty damn funny when you think about it. And the big friend of his, we ran into him running out of the woods, screaming like a little girl."

"I'm sorry. Go ahead and read a little and I'll be quiet."

I flipped open the first page and rubbed my temples with my thumbs as I had to restart a few times. I may not be a good writer but I knew excellent scribing and I knew crap rambling when I read it and his was the worst I had ever seen. It made my writing look like Cormac McCarthy. I was five pages into it and he was still describing the detective's office; ohhh—the agony.

I paused and wiped the sweat off my forehead and swallowed a mouthful of water hoping there was arsenic in it that would end this torture. I felt like this was some kind of cruel joke and candid camera was about to walk in at any moment.

"Pretty good, eh?"

"Words can't describe it," I replied, going back to my painful reading. When I finished the first ten pages I set the plagued paper back in the middle of the table. "What if I refuse?"

"Well, well. Another victim willing to test my power," he cackled. He picked up the blue rubber band and placed an end in each clenched fist, stretching it back and forth while smiling. "I will tell you that you will go to the Federal Prison in Danbury and it's chuck full of hardcore ladies. A cute chick like you'll make a nice trophy wife for some four hundred pound Beulah."

"You can't do that."

"Oh, yes I can." He took the rubber band off and reached into his inner jacket pocket, pulling out his identification, opening it and sliding it across the table. "I'm the Federal Bureau of Investigation. I do whatever I want and this badge gives me the power. I would hate to think what would come of that cute little daughter of yours. She may end up in foster care, with some..."

"You bastard!"

"Yes, but I'm a hired bastard, though I'd like to be a free-agent bastard."

"You're lucky you have my daughter as a bargaining chip or I'd tell you to take this manuscript and stick it up your pie hole."

"Ouch. Listen. I have been published before—look." He slid a slim paperback across the table and I read the title.

Out of Bullets.

"You see that was the first installment in the detective series. Then the next one here is *Out of Ammo*. It's the continuation. Unforeseen circumstances forced me to self-publish. If Hollywood ever smartens up and makes it into a movie, it could be huge. Someone could win an Academy Award."

I opened the book and there was no publisher listed. "A vanity press?" I asked, holding the book on the corner as if it were contagious.

"I had that printed locally, paid for it out of my retirement fund.

You show that to your agent and she'll sign me up for sure. Then we'll both be New York Times best selling authors."

"Okay, what if I accept but my agent doesn't?"

"No deal, Daisy, baby. You use your leverage like I'm using mine. You tell that agent of yours that she takes me on or no second book, besides, once she takes the time to read my stuff, it won't matter, she'll love it. Know what I'm sayin'?"

"You got a deal," I mumbled, looking at the floor. I had to do this to make sure my little girl didn't turn out to be a plagiaristic, lying, murderer like me. I never felt so ashamed of anything in all my life.

"Here you are. You're free to go," he smirked. He handed me his first book, his new manuscript, and his business card. "Once I get my book deal, I'll hand over these tapes to you and you're off the hook."

"Wait a minute. You said all I had to do was get you an agent. I can't control a publisher."

"That won't be a problem once your agent reads it," he boasted.

I stood up and he bounded around the table with his hand out. I shook it and it was cold and moist. He shook my arm up and down vigorously and pulled me in so close that I could smell his trout breath, and see my reflection in his bulging eyes.

"This book deal will finally get me out of this hellhole assignment. I can't thank you enough for liking my writing. I look forward to working with you. Who knows, I might put your name in the acknowledgements in the front of my book when it's published. You know it's kinda hilarious baby, how all those people got gold fever and died for a worthless chunk of gold—fools gold. You became a killin' broad for a ten cent chunk of sod."

I stepped out into the office wanting to smash Agent Harrisson's face with his crappy manuscript.

The government drones were gathered around listening to Buttercup sing, "Row, row, row, your boat." She was belting the song out while standing on the top of a desk looking like Shirley Temple, the agents were all smiling at her.

"Mommy, I was singing."

"I know, honey. It was beautiful."

Chapter 34

Buttercup Cornelia Loomis

I watched Utica disappear out of the back window as we headed for Waterville. I didn't know what I was going to do about the crappy manuscript of Agent Harrisson. I set it on the seat on the other side of Buttercup.

The two agents never spoke another word to us even when Buttercup recited, "Fatty and skinny went to bed. Fatty rolled over and skinny was dead."

My daughter straddled my knee to see the view out the window as we went through the quaint village of Clinton, where Cornelia Loomis would've fit in well with her New England charm. I was proud my daughter would continue the bloodline of the nefarious crime family. I even changed my last name; now I wanted to be a Loomis. I was sure my new name would evoke fear in the Mohawk Valley townies and I was fine with that. I knew my father would be thrilled with my part of the Loomis history.

When we pulled into the long, steep, dirt driveway that led up to my house, there was a black pickup truck parked in front. Blanche and Don were sitting on the front steps with their chins in their hands, looking bored.

"Please let me off here."

The agents stopped the car and we began to walk up the driveway. They pulled away with Buttercup yelling "bye" as the dust engulfed us. She walked slowly up the driveway picking up rocks on the way. She picked and pitched handful after handful until she found a smooth white stone that she held onto like it was gold.

"Look at this one, Mommy." She held it out on her little palm.

I got down on one knee. "Let me see." I picked it up and poked it with my finger. "This looks like a keeper sweetie. Hang onto it and we'll put it in your collection."

I stood back up, pulled an unlit cigarillo from my breast pocket, and gnawed on it.

"Where were you?" Blanche demanded standing up and tapping her cheap shoes on my cobblestone walk. "We been here watching this scumbag while you're out gallivanting with a couple of old men."

I ignored her and went over to the artist, a white dude, with black dreadlocks, a hoop piercing one eyebrow, and tattoos on both arms. Little did she know he was a gifted art student who went to nearby Utica College and was the son of one of the richest computer geeks in the world. He was standing in front of a white canvas that covered his work.

I had commissioned Dijon to sculpt me a statue to sit in front of my library. I picked up Daisy and everyone walked over to see what was under the canvas.

"Viola!" announced Dijon, pulling the canvas off the statue of Doodle that he made from my description, as all the photographs I had of the old boy were destroyed in the fire.

"That's ugly," blurted Don.

"What in the hell is that?" asked Glenn.

"You are too much like your father," snarled Blanche.

"Neato," yelled Buttercup.

"You bet your little self its neato," agreed Dijon. He rolled up the canvas and pitched it through the opened window of his truck.

"Well, everyone, since this is the Doodle Library, I wanted a memorial to its namesake." I loved the gray molded statue of Doodle holding his head up looking proud and strong. Dijon had captured the imperfect kitty with his snaggletooth and raggedy appearance. I couldn't have been happier.

Dijon asked for help lifting the statue off the flatbed and got a quick excuse from Glenn. Don waved his hand and rolled his eyes, so I threw Harrisson's crappy manuscript onto the driveway and helped Dijon lift the statue and place it right next to the front entrance of my library. Then, the talented artist left with a check in his hand that my family drooled over as I wrote it. I loved the superiority money had given me over them and for a moment I forgot the stupid Harrisson deal, and snickered under my breath, for I had not given these lowlifes a single red cent. They didn't know that an attorney would assure they never would get a penny upon my death. I left everything to my little girl.

"I'm hungry," whined Don. He was rubbing his stomach, his lips pouting downward. He was closing in on forty and still acted like he was ten.

"Me too. Can we get out of here? I hate the stench of the swamp," complained Glenn. He was waving his bony hand in front of his face, his comb-over wilting in the heat, sliding down his greasy forehead.

"You two go ahead and come back to pick me up when you're done," said Blanche, looking at her watch. I'd like to visit with my daughter and granddaughter for awhile. The guys peeled out and she called, "Come here, Blanche," and held out her hand.

"I told you before her name's not Blanche, Blanche." I was so angry with my mother. "Her name's Buttercup Cornelia Loomis."

"Ugh. You know I've had to live with that stupid name that your father picked for you off of a girly calendar, and now my granddaughter's the laughingstock of the entire area with that stupid, pitiful name. Just pathetic—really.

"You know that this house would be worth more if you removed that old trailer? I would have a hard time selling this with that tin can next door. Oh, well. By the way I've been thinking. I think it's high time you called me mother."

I wanted to take my boot off and vomit in it. She had been dropping hints that she wanted me to give her some money and I was starting to sense that I might have bumped past her beloved Don on her relationship totem pole.

"Fine—Mother. Watch your granddaughter for a minute while I go into the house and get a present I have for her."

Buttercup was picking through the grass, probably seeking out grasshoppers. She loved to grab them by their wings and flip them upside down, she'd laugh at the flailing legs. Then she'd set them on my palm and they'd kick with those powerful back legs and disappear back into their surroundings.

"Mommy," she said, "I don't got the grasshopper no more."

"Don't got?" Blanche blurted out as she lit a new smoke with the lit stub of the old one hanging crookedly off her lip. She arched her eyebrow. "She sure sounds like the daughter of an educated woman."

"Blanche, please!"

I went into the library and set Harrisson's manuscript down. It shouldn't have the honor to be placed alongside the fine literature that I'd hand picked. I thought that if I did indeed pull off Harrisson's request, I'd be just like Pearl Hart, the last person in America to rob a stagecoach. I'd be the scoundrel of the publishing world.

I picked a book off the shelf and cracked open the new edition, closed my eyes, and smelled the fresh ink. It reminded me of when I was a child and books were the key to everything. And no science fiction, absolutely no science fiction. I had nothing against H.G. Wells, he just wasn't invited to this party. What a rush to be able to read what I chose. To have the power to recommend to others what to read. That was real power. Educated power.

I loved my life now that I had a daughter—a friend to mentor and love. I was thrilled that I had a wine cellar filled with my Lucas Vineyards' Tug Boat Red, my over-stuffed reading chair was strategically placed in front of my red brick fireplace. A real working fireplace with split wood logs and creosote up the flu. No gas-powered or artificial fireplace would ever do for me. I had everything I had ever wanted, and I was feeling that my life was complete, serendipitous, that all my dreams were finally reality. All my nightmares were memories. I was in love with my life now... content, happy, at peace with God again. Well, except for the interloper Harrison.

I went upstairs to my bedroom. I had bought something for Buttercup a year earlier and wanted to give it to her now because she was finally ready for it. I looked around me and wished I had my father with me to see this. He'd be wearing his bowler, smiling. I pulled a whittling starter kit out from under my bed. I opened the lid and took out a small piece of basswood and rubbed my thumb across it. I knew Buttercup would be thrilled for she loved to watch me when I was whittling. I had begun to rebuild my ark and now we could save the kingdom together.

I went over to the end table and there sat my bowler with a deep cut in it. Buttercup's safety scissors were next to the hat. I felt myself getting upset. I could feel the blood boiling in my veins. This violation was worse than the incident with Johnson.

"Mommy. Look. I got one," Buttercup came running in to show me something. I turned and she was smiling with her hands cupped together.

"Why did you do this?" I pointed to the bowler that had been damaged.

"I dunno."

I slapped her across the face. She stepped back and fell on her rear end, losing the grasshopper that jumped past me. As soon as it happened I knew I had made a mistake.

"Buttercup. Sweetie. I'm..." It was too late for she ran out of the room screaming, tears running down her face. Blanche came in hugging her a second later.

"You're a terrible mother. How dare you slap your child," she screamed. Blanche turned and left me alone with my shame.

I went and picked up my father's hat that I had planned on passing down to my daughter. I examined the cut and noticed that there was something peculiar about the inside fabric. I tore open the hat, and inside was the edge of what looked like an animal skin so I tugged and another pelt came out that had the same calligraphy written on it as the one Shane had. Was it the true map that my father referred to?

I never was told, or asked my father where he acquired the bowler. This might've been Wash's own hat for all I knew. It was really old and faded. This could be the real map to the real gold.

I looked out the window and I saw my sweet girl heading down the knob, a good half mile away, speeding towards Nine Mile Swamp. I dropped the hat and map, knocking over the whittling kit as I sped by. The wooden animals and the knife crashed on my hardwood floor as I ran out of the room and down the stairs.

As I bolted out the front door, I saw Blanche buffing her nails with an emery board, not even looking up as I sprinted past her. I ran down the hill but couldn't see Buttercup. She had disappeared into the swamp.

Epilogue

While fictitious, this story is loosely based on the real Loomis Gang, who really were the single largest family crime syndicate in nineteenth century America.

The history of the Loomis Gang deserves to be well known and I hope this book will enlighten and interest you on the adventures of the smartest gang in the history of the United States. Nobody can know the true daily interactions of the Loomis Gang for the truth has been whisked away with time.

Today, the knob that served as the perch of the Loomis homestead remains bald and unoccupied. The Loomis home was never rebuilt after Sheriff Filkins burned it to the ground. Wash's ghost is said to walk the fringes of Loomis knob.

The lost treasure of Wash Loomis is still rumored to be hidden in Nine Mile Swamp.

For further reading, I recommend: *The Loomis Gang*, by George W. Walter, and *Frontier Justice: The Rise and Fall of the Loomis Gang*, by E. Fuller Torrey, M.D., and the documentary film "The Loomis Gang" by Brian Peter Falk if you are interested in learning more about on the antics of this criminal empire in Upstate New York.

About the Author

photo by Kelly Sweeney-Webster

Dennis Webster is a graduate of Oriskany High School and Utica College. He was born, lives, works and plays in the foothills of the Adirondack Mountains—the Mohawk Valley of Central New York. He resides in a modest home with his wife, three children and one howling beagle.

You can contact the author through e-mail: dennis66@adelphia.net or at his official website: www.denniswebster.com. *Daisy Daring and the Quest For the Loomis Gang Gold* is Dennis' first novel.